A HIGHLANDER'S BRIDE

The Mackenzies of Castle Leod
Book 1

Callie Hutton

ARE YOU SIGNED UP FOR DRAGONBLADE'S BLOG?

You'll get the latest news and information on exclusive giveaways, exclusive excerpts, coming releases, sales, free books, cover reveals and more.

Check out our complete list of authors, too!

No spam, no junk. That's a promise!

Sign Up Here

www.dragonbladepublishing.com

Dearest Reader;

Thank you for your support of a small press. At Dragonblade Publishing, we strive to bring you the highest quality Historical Romance from some of the best authors in the business. Without your support, there is no 'us', so we sincerely hope you adore these stories and find some new favorite authors along the way.

Happy Reading!

CEO, Dragonblade Publishing

**Additional Dragonblade books by
Author Callie Hutton**

The Mackenzies of Castle Leod
A Highlander's Bride (Book 1)
A Highlander's Vow (Book 2)

The Lyon's Den Series
The Lyon and the Lass

CHAPTER ONE

Spring, 1729
Foulis Castle, Scotland

BETH MUNRO STOOD with her mother on the drawbridge of Foulis Castle, waving at the last one of her sisters to leave with her husband and bairns.

Her mam patted the corner of her eyes and sighed. "I'm always sorry to see my grandchildren leave."

Beth shook her head and shivered. "No' me."

When her mam leaned back and looked at her in a shocked manner, Beth said, "Doona get me wrong. I love the little ones when they come to visit, but having all three of my sisters and their numerous bairns at one time is quite overwhelming."

"'Twas my birthday! And they are so sweet!" her mam said as she wrapped her arm around Beth's waist and walked them toward the keep.

"Aye. Little David was verra sweet when he smeared honey all over the floor in front of the table in the kitchen. Our poor cook, Daisy, was beside herself as she tried to cook the evening meal and her feet kept sticking to the floor. She even lost one of her shoes and she swears David's sweet little sister, Aileen took it."

Her fool mam had the nerve to laugh.

"And Da didn't appear too amused when he found yer three oldest sweet grandchildren had pulled all the books off the library shelves and piled them near the door so he couldn't get in and had to climb through the window to rescue them."

"They dinna mean any harm, they're just bairns." Mam turned toward the kitchen. "I will go smooth Daisy down and will offer to purchase her new shoes in the village tomorrow."

Beth smirked. "'Twould be nice to sell yer grandchildren to pay for the shoes."

Mam turned to her. "I doona understand ye, Beth. Most women love the idea of raising bairns. Ye ken I was so happy with my four daughters."

"Aye. Three of yer daughters married and produced bairns at an alarming rate whose mission in life is to torture us."

She gave a sigh. "I would like to see ye settled with bairns of yer own, ye ken."

Beth leaned over and kissed her much-too-patient mam on the cheek. "With eight grandchildren, and another on the way, ye have enough to keep ye busy. If I were foolish enough to marry, the number of little devils would probably double."

She shook her head and waved her finger in the air. "Ye may change yer mind one day, daughter."

Beth smiled. "Mam, ye're hopeless."

Her mam headed to the kitchen to soothe the cook and Beth returned to her bedchamber. 'Twas so peaceful, even though her niece Ada had spilled all of her new box of bathing powder over the floor.

It dinna matter because they were gone and she had her peace and quiet back. Just her, her books, garden, and charity work in the village. She loved her life and was more than happy that with all the confusion in their life, her da had forgotten about her not having a husband, so she enjoyed her single life and had no desire for things to change.

Castle Leod, Scotland

ABRAHAM MACKENZIE, ONE of the Clan Elder Advisors, probably as old as the one in the Bible, sat back, his hands on the table, tapping the wood with his wrinkled finger. "'Tis yer duty and ye ken it. If ye die tomorrow, there is no one to take yer place."

"I have no intention of dying tomorrow, I have too much to do." Daniel Mackenzie, Clan Chief of the Mackenzies sat back and crossed his arms over his chest. "We are at peace. Castle Leod is well protected as are the other castles on the Mackenzie lands and I have no reason to believe I will be deserting this world anytime soon."

Morgan, another advisor leaned forward and after glancing at the other two advisors, looked Daniel directly in the eyes. "It appears ye no longer have time to put this off."

Daniel uncrossed his arms and stared at the man. "What are ye talking about?"

Morgan cleared his throat and pulled a document from his pouch and laid it on the table in front of them. "We have an order here from our king."

Daniel straightened in his chair. "If an order was sent by King George II to the Mackenzie Clan Chief—which is me—I should have been the one to receive it."

Abraham leaned forward. "The messenger was told to give the order to the Mackenzie advisors to present it to the laird."

Daniel glared at them, one at a time. "I think ye are making this up to get yer own way."

Morgan pushed the document across the table. The seal had been broken, but there was no doubt it was the king's seal. Daniel opened it and saw his future there on the paper.

The king had chosen two lasses to appear at Castle Leod for the purpose of Clan Chief, Laird Daniel Mackenzie, to arrange to marry one of them by the Feast of Beltane.

Apparently trying to soothe Daniel's apparent rising anger, Abraham said, "I understand yer reluctance, lad. Marriage is a big step. However, ye will notice," he gestured toward the king's order, "that the two lasses he chose are both from clans important to our lands. Either one will make an important alliance with us."

Daniel looked at the parchment again. It appeared King George II had already invited Lady Alice Chisholm and Lady Beth Munro and their parents to Castle Leod for him to look over.

Daniel sat stunned, staring at the three men. "The king invited two lass's families to visit us so I can *look them over?*"

Looking a tad uncomfortable, Abraham nodded. "Aye."

He was truly without words. "And I assume The Munro and The Chisholm have already responded?"

Richard, the third member of the group nodded. "Aye. They are on their way now. Lady Beth Munro, and her parents Laird and Lady Munro and Lady Alice Chisholm, and her parents, Laird and Lady Chisholm."

Daniel dropped his head in his hands. "Why dinna ye ask me first?"

Richard, another clan advisor shrugged. "Because we had no choice." He gestured to the king's order, "and we kenned ye would say 'nay' if given a choice."

"*St. Agnes's mustache!* Of course I would have said *nay*. He makes this appear as if I were purchasing a horse, looking two of them over."

Morgan drew himself up. "The mon is our king and an order has come directly from him. As yer advisors, we must make sure ye do yer duty."

Since the lasses were already on the way, with one expecting to return home with a betrothal agreement, there wasn't much he could do. "Do the lasses ken there are two of them?"

Richard nodded. "Ye dinna take the time to read the entire missive from the king. He sent an invitation to The Chisholm and The Munro, letting them know there were two lasses selected."

Morgan shrugged. "I guess His Majesty wanted to give ye a choice."

"Please speak truthfully, Morgan. I have no choice. Beltane is not far off and there are two lasses coming here with their parents hoping to become the wife of the Mackenzie Clan Chief."

Too unsettled at this news, he slapped his hands on the table and stood. "I have work to do."

The three *idjit* advisors smiled and nodded at each other. If it weren't for the king's seal he would have been certain they'd made this up.

"I HAVE SOME news for ye, Beth."

Her dad sat in the most comfortable chair in his solar. He waved to the one on his right. Her mam sat in the other chair. She couldn't imagine what would require such a formal meeting with her parents. They didn't look distressed so 'twas apparently not bad news. In fact, after taking a second notice, her da was smiling.

But her mam's hands were fidgeting in her lap.

"What is this news?" She smiled at her da who had always been the best of men. Even though he had four daughters, he always seemed to offer her a bit more of himself. Especially now with Beth being the only offspring left.

"The king may have found a husband for ye."

Beth sat very still and just stared at him. Licking her dry lips, she said, "I doona understand, Da. I haven't lost one. Nor do I want one to lose."

He continued to smile and the fidgeting in her mam's lap grew alarmingly frantic.

She shook her head and offered her best smile to her da. "'Tis a joke, aye, Da?" She waved her finger at him. "Ye ken I ne'er wanted to marry. Ye have all these daughters, and trying to keep up with all their bairns may have mixed ye up. I am Beth—yer youngest. And the one who will take care of ye and Mam when ye grow old."

"Nay, lass. Mam and I will be verra content in our old age if all our offspring are happily married."

Beth sniffed. "I doona assign the word 'married' with 'happily'."

Her da looked over at her mam. "Jean, please explain to our daughter how happy marriage is."

Twisting her fingers, her mam said, "'Tis verra happy, dear."

"Well then, that's quite an enthusiastic response." She was actually sweating by now because she had the very uncomfortable feeling her parents were serious.

Taking a deep breath, she asked, "How does the king fit into this? Who is this husband he *found* for me? Hiding under a bush in the garden? If so, I'll borrow your gun and shoot him."

Her da straightened in his chair. "Now I will have no disrespect from ye, lass. 'Tis the Clan Chief of the Mackenzies, a very strong clan."

She was horrified. "Isn't The Mackenzie in his sixth decade?" 'Twas bad enough to be shoved off onto some unknown man, but to one older than her da turned her stomach.

"Nay, the old laird died over two years ago. His son, who is about five and twenty years, is the laird."

When Beth didn't seem impressed, her mam turned to her da. "Stephen, tell her about the other lass."

Beth's brows shot to her hairline. "Other lass? Is the laird wanting to marry two women?" She turned to her mam. "Does the Church allow that?"

Her da waved her comment away. "Nay, daughter, calm yerself. There is another lass and her family who will also be at the castle. The king arranged for two lasses to attend so the laird can have his pick." He sat back, his hands crossed over his middle, looking very satisfied with himself.

Anger shot through her as Beth jumped from her chair. "Are ye telling me that the king has ordered me to be paraded before some laird I ne'er saw, and then be embarrassed by being compared to another lass like he was buying a *horse*?" She took a breath. "Should I show him my teeth, then?"

Her da stood and looked over at her mam. "Jean, ye should be dealing with this anyway." He turned to Beth. "Pack what ye need. We leave in the morning for Castle Leod." With those words resounding in the room, he left, closing the door with more enthusiasm than was necessary.

Beth turned to her mam. "Please tell me this was all a nightmare that I will soon awaken from."

Her mam walked to her and put her arm around her shoulders, hugging her close. "'Twon't be so bad."

"But Mam, I ne'er wanted to get married. We've spoken of this before. Let my sisters add to the Munro population."

Mam moved her forward. "I ken that, dear, but ye must have kenned that one day it would happen. Laird's daughters are no' allowed to remain single. They must bring alliances and coin to their families."

Beth leaned back and looked at her mam. "Da has made three alliances with my sisters' marriages. How many does he need?"

Mam shook her head as they started up the stairs to the bedchamber floor. "'Tis the king's order, Beth." She stopped halfway up the stairs and turned. "Ye say ye will remain here to take care of us in our old age. Who will take care of ye in yer old age?"

DANIEL WOKE TO the sound of someone yelling. "Laird!"

He'd spent the prior night drinking away his anger, which had done nothing except make him oversleep and awaken with a pounding head and a stomach ready to bring up whatever it was he'd last eaten. Along with the whisky.

He threw off the bedcovers and pulled his braies on, slipping into his *léine* as he strode to the door and out into the hall.

A young lad who Daniel remembered as being the son of one of the stable masters raced up to him, out of breath. "Laird, they need ye in the stables. One of the horses broke out of his stall and ran o'er a groom."

They both ran from the keep with Daniel yelling to the closest guard. "Get the healer and have her meet us at the stables."

There seemed to be a dozen guardsmen huddled at the entrance to the stable. "All of ye get back to the lists and keep training."

Daniel made his way through the crowd, now breaking up, and walked to the man lying on the ground, with Brendan, the head stable master hovering over him.

"How is he?" Daniel asked.

"I'm no' sure, Laird. The horse bumped him on the shoulder and then stepped on his leg as he ran from the stable."

He nodded and bent down alongside the man. Daniel didn't want to turn him over in case it damaged him further. "Who is he?"

"Ian Mackenzie, Laird," Brendan said.

Before Daniel had a chance to ask anything else, the healer, Emma, hurried up to him, clutching her ever-present basket of medicants. "What happened here?"

Daniel nodded to Brendan to explain to the lass.

After learning about the mishap and examining him, she ordered him to be taken to one of the bed chambers so she could help him.

Daniel authorized the use of one of the keep bedchambers. The men moved Ian onto a large board and they carried him upstairs with Daniel leading the way. Once the man was settled and Emma attending him, Daniel downed a mug of ale, then went to his own bedchamber, washed and dressed for the day.

He had plans to visit one of the bothies who were having problems with leakage. He ordered a wagon with supplies on it so he and the owner, John, could fix the problem if it wasn't too bad. Since this was the first he'd heard about it, he assumed they could quickly mend it.

'Twas a cloudy day, which only added to the depression of his overindulgence and lack of enthusiasm for the king's edict. When he got to the bothy, he found several of other men from the village had already started on the roof. With them all working silently, they got the leakage and other problems the man was having fixed. It took longer than Daniel had expected and it was almost dark when he left the bothy.

After sweating out the alcohol from his body as he made his way through the job, Daniel decided to take advantage of the light from the full moon so he went to the loch and, stripping off his clothes, dove into the cold water. He swam for about a half hour and then climbed out, dried himself with his *léine*, then slid his braies on and headed back to the keep.

He wanted nothing more than a quick meal in the kitchen and a good night's sleep.

An unknown carriage sat in front of the stable. He walked up to Lewis, the man who was now taking Ian's place until the man was able to return to work. That reminded Daniel that he needed to look in on Ian to see how the man was faring. When he'd first seen him, he hadn't looked too bad, but it was hard to tell these things without a healer's report which he would receive soon.

"Whose carriage is this?" Daniel asked Lewis.

"Laird Munro, his wife and daughter arrived while ye were gone. I think Louise greeted them in yer place and led them to the keep."

Daniel nodded. So, one of the lasses had arrived. It must have been Lady Beth Munro. He knew nothing about her, except that right now she was housed in one of the bedchambers in the castle.

He strode to the outer bailey where he found his chatelaine, Louise, directing men to unload a wagon that must have belonged to the Munro family.

"There ye are, laird. Ye weren't here to meet yer guests," Louise said, looking a tad put out.

"Nay. I was seeing to the injury of one of our men, then spent the rest of the day fixing John's bothy so he and his wife and bairns won't have to sleep under trees if it rains."

"Did ye ken they were coming?" She gestured toward the carriage that was now being brought to the stables.

"Aye and nay. The king has ordered two lasses and their parents to Castle Leod for the purpose of me selecting one to marry."

Louise sucked in a breath and placed her hand on her chest. "So soon. Dinna the king give ye time to prepare?"

Daniel shook his head. "Nay. I only found out about it yesterday."

The chatelaine shook her head, placing her hands on her middle. She sniffed, and rightly so, since she was the one who had to provide for guests without prior notice and the laird present. "I sent them up to their bedchambers to refresh themselves before we have supper, which will be verra soon."

There went his plans for a quick supper and a comfortable bed. He nodded. "I will change and go to the great hall in time to greet them when they come down."

Daniel took a deep breath.

And now it begins.

CHAPTER TWO

Three days before
Foulis Castle

B ETH LOOKED AROUND the bedchamber she'd slept in for as long as she could remember, the trunks full of the lovely gowns her mam had made for her to bring to the "bride-to-be" auction. She and another lass would be paraded before some arrogant, obnoxious laird for *his choice*. Every time she thought about it, she grew angrier.

She sat on the bed, her chin resting on her fist. She couldn't believe her da, who had loved her dearly all her life, had agreed to this.

She gave a great sigh, then after a minute or so, a smile broke out on her face. Slowly she sat up and laughed, then laughed harder. Yes, she would do it! It would definitely cause some problems for her, but it would be worth it if she turned the laird's eyes to the other lass, whoever she might be.

She raced to her wardrobe and began pulling out her old gowns, aprons ready for the trash, and her old shredded worn cape.

Next, she took a trip to the kitchen to speak with their cook, Daisy, then she went to the bedchamber where her mam stored the family's old clothes to give to the unfortunate in the village. She scooped up knitting needles that sat in her room along with an unused ball of yarn.

Happy with her work, and laughing until the tears ran down her cheeks, she blew out the candle and settled into bed. Now she was looking forward to her visit to Castle Leod. This arrogant laird was in for some surprises.

The next morning, she greeted her parents in the great hall to break her fast.

"Good morning, daughter. Are ye ready to leave as soon as we are finished here?" Her da looked expectantly at her.

She shrugged. "Since I have no choice, aye I am ready."

Her mam wiped her mouth with a piece of linen. "Ye might verra well enjoy yourself, daughter. I hear the laird is quite handsome and verra friendly."

She huffed. With a man in the laird's position "very friendly" usually meant he was chasing the lasses in his employ and warming his bed with them.

The ride to Castle Leod from her home took a little less than two full days. Fortunately, her da knew of an inn where they stayed so she wasn't forced to sleep in the carriage or, worse, on the ground like her da said the guardsmen with them would do.

Castle Leod was only a half day ride from where her sister, Lady Alisa Grant, lived with her husband and bairns. She asked her da about stopping for a visit, but he was anxious to please the king and go to Castle Leod straightaway.

When they arrived at Castle Leod, she breathed a sigh of relief when a woman who introduced herself as Louise Mackenzie, the chatelaine, greeted them and said the laird was in the village solving some sort of problem and would be down shortly to greet them.

They were shown to their bedchambers which were right next to each other. She examined the room she'd been assigned. The walls were painted white, a plush carpet covered the floor and the bed was large and looked comfortable with a colorful bed covering and hangings. It all looked so cozy that she almost forgot what her visit here was all about. She didn't want to admire the room or feel comfortable in the bed.

She rested her elbows on the ledge of the glass window and studied the grounds surrounding the castle in the bright moonlight, which cast dips and shadows over the area of valleys and hills surrounding it.

Her mam knocked and entered the room. "This is a lovely chamber. I notice all the rooms we passed looked clean and well-decorated."

She narrowed her eyes at her mam. "Aye. 'Tis a nice Keep."

"Ye could be Lady of the Manor here." Her mam studied the room and Beth could swear she was picturing little bairns running around the area, creating havoc.

Just the thought of it made Beth cringe. *Lady of the Manor* meant bearing those bairns and listening to them as they cried and kicked and screamed over a biscuit. Or tried their best to kill each other.

Or themselves.

She shook her head to remove the image as her mam said, "I believe they will be serving supper in about an hour."

"I am weary from the trip, so I think I will request a tray in my room, and a hot bath. What I need is a good night's sleep."

"That seems fine, dear. 'Twill will give ye time to recover from our journey and look yer best when ye meet the laird in the morning."

That's what her mother thought, anyway. Beth smiled to herself. "Aye, Mam. I will see ye in the morning."

DANIEL AWOKE THE next day with a sinking feeling in his stomach. When he'd finished supper with Laird and Lady Munro the night before, he'd been grateful when Lady Munro excused herself and Laird Munro shortly thereafter.

Their conversation had been a bit stiff with Lady Beth missing. Were he not the host, he would have gone with his plan to have a quick supper and bed.

He'd headed to his solar and sat in his well-worn, comfortable chair, linking his fingers on his stomach, and thought about what he was soon to face. He had assumed he would eventually get used to this foolish idea the king had come up with, but he still was angry about it.

The worst part was the king's inviting two young ladies to visit at the same time. It did make it seem as if he was looking over items to purchase. The more he thought about the next morning, the more annoyed he became with the interfering man, king or not.

Not happy about what he was facing, but knowing marriage was something necessary for a laird, he would have preferred to do it in his own time and in his own way. And with his own choice. This farce had the pretense of choice but in truth, gave none at all. It was an insult.

Bringing his thoughts back to the present, he headed to the great hall to see Laird and Lady Munro sitting on the dais. There was no young lass in sight. He walked up to them and bowed. "Good morn, my Laird, my Lady, I hope ye had a pleasant sleep?"

The laird stood. "Good morn to ye as well. I remembered after we parted last evening that ye were at the clans' competition last year."

Daniel nodded. "Aye myself and Gregory, my cousin as well as my second-in-command, always enter the events."

"Ye did well at the competition. I was quite how taken with how ye and Gregory took most of the awards."

Daniel moved to the seat next to Lady Munro. She turned to him with the bright smile of a mother trying to marry off one of her offspring. It was one he'd seen before and had always successfully avoided, until now. "'Tis sorry I am that Lady Beth is no' here yet, but when I stopped by her bedchamber a little while ago, she said she would be down shortly."

Daniel waved to one of the kitchen lasses who took a peek in the room. "Lass, please bring me some ale." He turned to the laird. "Would ye or yer wife like a refill? Or something else to drink?"

"Nay, yer chatelaine was verra gracious. She is a lovely lass."

The young maid dipped and left for the kitchen.

Just then Lady Munro sucked in a deep breath as she stared across the room, her hand on her chest, her eyes wide.

He looked where she was gaping at a young lass shuffling toward them. She was quite plump and was dressed in the ugliest dress he'd ever seen. Her hair was pulled back in a tight bun at the back of her head. She wore spectacles and when he looked down at her feet as she hobbled along, she was wearing what looked like lad's shoes that were apparently too large for her.

She carried a ball of yarn and two knitting needles. She walked up to them and dipped. "Good morn, Laird."

Lady Munro seemed to recover herself, but she glared at her daughter. "Laird, this is my daughter, Lady Beth Munro." It sounded like she was choking trying to get the words out.

Laird Munro scowled at the lass, so Daniel assumed this was not her normal attire. He squelched the desire to laugh. 'Twas obvious this lass was not interested in him, or marriage to him.

"Good morn, Lady Beth. I am glad ye have joined us."

She nodded and sat in the seat next to him to which he pointed. She stumbled in her shoes as she reached the seat. He held his hand out to help her.

The lass pushed her spectacles, which kept sliding down, up on her nose. She wiggled it, and he was not sure if she was trying to keep the spectacles on or if her nose itched. He was having a very hard time keeping from laughing at the lass's antics. Meanwhile, it appeared her da was about to suffer apoplexy and her mam kept taking deep breaths.

"Would ye care to remove yer shawl, Lady Beth? Unless ye are cold?" His voice was choked with laughter, but since her parents seemed so distressed, he did his best to hold it in.

Lady Beth drew it closer. "Nay. I am verra cold." She reached out and filled her plate with the offerings from the platter on the table. She began to eat, and after swallowing each piece of food she wiped her mouth on her sleeve.

Lady Munro groaned.

Once Lady Beth had gobbled her food down, she picked up her knitting needles and began to attempt to knit, but it was apparent she had no idea how to do it.

Conversation continued around her, with the lass not contributing at all. Her mam tried several times to get her into the conversation, but each time the lass merely grunted like an animal and continued to clack and click her needles as she created knots in her yarn.

He had never been so entertained in his life. This lass apparently had no problem expressing her likes and dislikes, even if it embarrassed her parents.

One of the guardsmen approached the table and spoke when Daniel looked at him. "Laird, the Chisholm family has arrived."

Lady Munro gasped and stood. She reached for her daughter's arm and pulled her up. "Excuse us, Laird, but my daughter and I need to have a conversation."

The woman practically dragged her daughter from the great hall and up the stairs. The lass's shoes fell off her feet, leaving one on the great hall floor and the other one at the bottom of the stairs.

About ten minutes after Lady Munro left hauling her daughter, a very large man, a very small woman and a young lass entered the great hall. Daniel stood. "Laird Chisholm, Lady Chisholm, welcome to Castle Leod."

The man nodded. "'Tis good to meet ye, Laird." His wife turned to her daughter and pulled her forward. "This is our daughter, Lady Alice Chisholm. I'm sure you'll find her to be a good wife for ye."

Well, then. Let us not beat around the bush.

He had one lass who was trying to do her best to not be selected as his wife and had dressed for the part, and another whose mam was most likely wanting a meeting with Louise to plan the wedding breakfast menu before he and her daughter had even exchanged a word.

Lady Alice offered a bleak smile, her eyes downcast. It appeared her enthusiasm didn't meet her mam's.

Trying to be a good host, he said, "Lady Alice, 'tis verra nice to meet ye."

Her mam poked her in the back. "Say something, lass."

She dipped and said, "Good morn, Laird."

Daniel turned to Lady Chisholm. "I assume ye would like to be shown to yer bedchambers to freshen up before ye join us?"

"Aye, we would like that, Laird," Lady Chisholm said.

Just then Lady Munro entered the great hall. "My daughter will be right down, Laird." She looked as though she had been involved in a wrestling match. Maybe this little fete the king had planned might be interesting after all.

"I CANNO' BELIEVE ye would embarrass yer da and me by arriving at the great hall dressed like this!"

Beth had never heard her mam speak to her in such an angry voice. Her face was red and she was still huffing from practically dragging her up the stairs to her bedchamber.

She waved her finger in Beth's face. "Ye will change into something appropriate for visiting with the Makenzie Laird. And fix yer hair and where did ye get the spectacles? And those horrible shoes? And wiping yer mouth on the sleeve of that hideous dress. And where did you get that dress?"

The poor woman dropped to the bed and placed her hand on her chest. "I think I'm about to faint."

Beth began to get concerned. "I'm sorry, Mam. I dinna mean to upset ye so. I just doona want the laird to pick me." She walked across the room to summon a maid. "I'll send for some tea while I change."

Her mother nodded and seemed to calm down. After asking for tea from the young lass who answered her call, she began to shimmy out of the four dresses she had on, in hopes of appearing too plump to appeal to the laird.

Her mam's eyes grew wide as she wiggled out of the clothing. She began to fan herself with her ever-present linen cloth. "I think instead of having that tea, I will go back to the great hall and greet The Chisholm and his wife and daughter."

Beth nodded and continued to untie the bodice of the last dress. Her mam turned as she reached the door. "And doona come downstairs dressed in any way that is no' your usual way to do so." With a sharp close of the door, she left the room.

Beth sat on the bed and closed her eyes. She hadn't thought her idea would work quickly, but now her parents were both angry and would probably keep a close eye on her.

The self-important laird seemed to be laughing at her the entire time. He was very handsome, but most likely knew it and planned to have her and the other lass fall all over him.

Not her.

She was not going to give up and allow herself to be presented along with another girl like champion horses to catch the laird's eye.

She pulled out an "acceptable" dress to wear, thinking about the laird. In truth, he was more handsome than any man she had ever known. He had wavy, deep red hair that made it almost to his shoulders. His arms bulged with muscles that rippled every time he moved. Once he stood to greet her when she arrived to break her fast in the great hall, all she could see was his muscular thighs and calves, covered by snug braies. She dragged her eyes away from the sight and found herself looking into his blue eyes which showed both mirth and cleverness.

Well, he won't use his cleverness on me.

After washing off the flour she'd gotten from their cook at Faulis Castle that she'd used to cover her freckles and make her appear sickly, and then fixing her hair in her usual manner, with the two sides braided, pulled back, and fastened at the back of her head, she gazed into the looking glass and sighed.

Although her family always told her differently, she'd never considered herself pretty, but she knew she didn't shatter mirrors. Hopefully, the other lass competing for this arrogant oaf would be very pretty and charming and he would select her right away. Then she could go back to her life as it was and how she wanted it to continue.

She dug out a pair of her own shoes from one of the trunks and slipped them on. Time again to face the man she was determined not to impress, even if he was the finest-looking man she'd ever seen.

She smiled; she had other methods that her parents didn't know about.

CHAPTER THREE

D ANIEL WAITED PATIENTLY for Lady Beth and his three more newly arrived guests to appear. Lady Munro seemed to have calmed down. "I want to apologize to ye, Laird. I doona ken what my daughter was thinking, but she will be down shortly in a presentable manner."

He smiled and nodded, quite interested to see what the lass looked like when she wasn't dressed like a verra old woman. He still had a hard time not laughing about it again, which, given Lady's Munro tense scowl was probably not a good idea.

A maid had picked up the discarded shoes and with Lady Monro's instructions had discarded them.

"Good morn again, Laird." Laird Chisholm, his wife and daughter all entered the great hall.

Daniel stood and waved to the bench where Laird and Lady Munro sat, along with Gregory. Daniel gestured toward his cousin. "May I introduce ye to Gregory Mackenzie."

They nodded at him and Daniel said, "Please have a seat and the servers will bring out food and drink."

Lady Chisholm pushed her daughter toward the very slight space between Daniel and Lady Munro, which had been Lady Beth's seat before her mam had towed her off. "Ye can sit next to the Laird, Alice. I'm sure he is interested in speaking with ye."

Daniel moved closer to Lady Munro, who shifted toward her

husband. The servers entered with food and began to serve.

Lady Alice was a pleasant-looking lass. Brown eyes, straight, light brown hair, and pale skin gave her a somewhat simple look. After being nudged in her side by her mam, the lass smiled at him, and when he smiled back she looked down at her plate.

"Ah, here she is," Lady Munro said.

Daniel looked up and his hand stopped right before he was to put a piece of cold meat into his mouth. The lass walking toward them was beautiful. Long, blond, wavy hair, deep blue eyes and rosy lips that were meant to kiss...only him.

When she smiled the room lit up. As she grew closer he saw the light band of freckles across her nose and cheeks. He put the piece of meat back on his plate and stood.

"Good morn, Lady Beth."

She grinned. "I believe we've already said that, Laird."

"Beth," her mam said under her breath, but loud enough for him and her daughter to hear.

She dipped and did not wipe the smile from her face which made him want to laugh out loud again. Daniel did the introductions between the Chisholm family and Lady Beth.

Before he could ask Lady Munro to move over some more, Lady Beth walked around the dais and sat next to her da.

"Lady Alice is verra adept at handling bairns," Lady Chisholm said, leaning over her husband and daughter to speak to him. Lady Alice looked startled for a moment.

"Indeed." He looked at the young lass who was once again staring at her food.

"Say something," Lady Chisholm whispered not too softly to her daughter.

"Um, aye, Laird, I have young cousins who I help my aunt with." The poor lass actually broke out in a sweat on her forehead.

Taking sympathy for the lass, Daniel turned to Lady Munro next to him. "Did ye find yer bedchamber satisfactory?"

"Aye. 'Tis verra nice. Thank ye so much for having us, Laird."

"I agree, Laird. 'Tis so nice of ye to have us." Lady Chisholm was not to be left out of the conversation.

Daniel leaned past Laird and Lady Munro. "Lady Beth, are ye finding yer bedchamber satisfactory?"

She looked startled that anyone was even speaking to her. She wiped her mouth with her linen and smiled. "Aye. 'Tis verra nice."

"Maybe after we break our fast, the ladies would like to take a walk in your lovely garden that I saw from my bedchamber window," Lady Chisholm said. He nodded to her since he didn't know what else to do with them. What he wanted to do was ride his horse, Atlas.

For hours.

However, he didn't know how adept at riding either young lady was.

Right now he would be on the lists, watching over the training along with Gregory, who had left them before Lady Beth had arrived for the second time.

"Ye seem to have a wonderful stable, Laird. Mayhap we could take a ride," Lady Beth said, almost as if she read his mind.

"Oh, I doona ride verra well, I'm afraid," Lady Alice said, mumbling to her plate.

"'Tis no problem, Laird. I am allergic to flowers so ye and Lady Alice can go for yer walk and with yer permission I'll use one of yer horses for a ride," Lady Beth said, actually looking relieved. So, she didn't want to spend time with him.

He would work on that, since the lass seemed to be pushing him away. Which only made him want to pull her back. Besides, she fascinated him. Based on her mam's reaction, the disguise she pulled on him was a surprise to her parents. He found it hilarious. Although her parents didn't seem to think so.

Seeing as how the lass had already captured his attention, she was certainly worth the challenge.

"Ye are no' allergic to flowers, daughter," Lady Munro said.

"Oh, aye. The last time I was in our garden, I sneezed forever and had to take to my bed."

"'Tis strange that I doona remember that." Lady Munro glared at her daughter, but didn't say anything else.

Daniel would bet his best horse Lady Beth never let anything put her to bed in the middle of the day. Except him, however, if he had any say in it.

So ye have already decided, then?

"Mayhap I can join ye tomorrow morning for a ride, Lady Beth. I like to go early since I generally have some problems to address with the clan during the day."

She nodded, a broad smile on her face. The lass thought she had won because she avoided a walk in the garden when she would have to speak with him? Nay. Maybe for today. However, he could come up with as many plans as she had. He was really looking forward to this visit now.

What Lady Beth didn't know was that, aye, he had already selected which lass he wanted for his wife. 'Twasn't a difficult choice. Lady Beth was beautiful, charming when she wasn't trying to be otherwise, would never bore him, would always challenge him, and bring life and humor into the castle and his life.

Also, he was already planning hours and hours in his bed running his hands over those lush curves and teaching her ways to bring pleasure to them both.

It was apparent, however, that Lady Beth was going to try her best to avoid a betrothal agreement. He needed to learn if there was another man standing in his way that held her heart back at Foulis Castle.

While Lady Alice seemed to be a sweet lass, she was much too shy and accommodating for him. A warrior did not do well with a woman who wasn't his equal in temperament, and Lady Beth surely was. He almost rubbed his hands with excitement and delight at how the chase would be this week with his guests.

He could not believe King George II did something right.

BETH CHANGED INTO her riding clothes and left the keep. She would have a free day enjoying the fresh air and riding over the hills and valleys outside of Castle Leod while Laird Mackenzie was stuck walking through the flower garden entertaining Lady Alice.

Although not pleased, her mam didn't try to stop her from riding. Feeling free for the first time since her da had told her about this visit, she passed the men training on the lists and waved briefly to a few of them who called out to her.

She made her way to the immense stables behind the keep. And a wonderful stable it was! The horses were well cared for, healthy, and appeared anxious for a run. The animal she was given, Tiger, fit her perfectly.

The stablemaster seemed reluctant to allow her to ride without permission from the laird, but she assured him Laird Mackenzie did, in fact, give her permission and she was quite capable of handling any animal he would present her with.

Since she had mentioned she'd like to take a ride, and The Mackenzie hadn't said anything against it, as far as she was concerned, that was permission.

So, she was now riding in the fresh air, far away from Laird Mackenzie and Lady Alice and the flowers she was interested in.

After a couple hours of riding, stopping a few times near a stream to water her horse and give the animal a rest, she spotted a village in the distance and decided to enjoy the rest of the day by taking a look at the vendors who had set up tables in the middle of the village green. She left her horse at the village stable with an assurance to the stablemaster that Laird Mackenzie had allowed her to ride one of his horses.

The bright smile she had cast at the blushing young man who assisted her had most likely helped, as well.

The air was beautiful, warm but with a bit of a chill. The

vendors were different than the ones that sold their wares in Foulis Castle.

She enjoyed a lovely sweet cake as she strolled along. She was tempted to enter the village tavern inn and have an ale, but she was reluctant to antagonize her parents further by doing such a thing if they discovered her misstep.

But 'twas nice enough to enjoy what was offered by the village vendors.

It seemed in no time at all that her stomach was growling, the sun was beginning its descent, and she was quite thirsty. Since no one seemed to be looking for her, and the vendors in the green had begun to pack up, she decided to enter the tavern inn, anyway. With luck she would be able to eat and drink an ale and make it in time to dress for supper, which her stomach did not want to wait for.

She was taking a sip of ale after enjoying a mutton pie when a voice she never really wanted to hear again said, "Lady Beth Munro, how verra nice to see ye here."

She groaned and closed her eyes. Laird Daniel Mackenzie drew out the chair at her table and sat. "If ye were hungry, our cook Jemima would have been happy to feed ye something before the evening supper."

Why was this man plaguing her? She wanted nothing to do with him, but every time she looked up, there he was, smirking at her.

Beth shrugged. "I dinna want to bother her."

He nodded at the lass who set down a mug of ale in front of him. "And ye took one of my horses to ride to the village."

She backed up and stared at him. "Was I no' allowed to do that? Aren't I one of yer guests? And I told ye I was going for a ride. Did ye think, then, that I would be riding a wagon wheel or one of yer chickens?"

He grinned. "Aye, while another of my guests and I were traipsing through the flower garden."

Beth shrugged. "I'm sure ye had a good time. I already told ye

I am allergic to flowers."

He waved at the server and asked for a refill of his ale. "Yer mam seems to think yer allergy to flowers is something new."

Her annoyance grew. Whatever was between her and her mam was none of his business. "Aye. It started just a few weeks ago." She continued to sip her ale and did her best to ignore him. After a few minutes she said, "Why are ye here?" She knew her mam would faint dead away if she heard the way she was speaking to the laird.

"I am here because my cousin, Gregory spotted ye heading toward the village and as my guest and with yer parents concerned about yer whereabouts I set out to bring ye safely home."

Beth sighed and ran her fingertip in a circle in a small puddle of ale. "I have a great deal of freedom at my home. The only reason they were concerned by my absence was because they wanted to make sure I was spending enough time with ye."

His brows rose. "And that doesn't please ye?"

Aye, the man was over-confident. Most likely he assumed she and Lady Alice would be fighting each other for his attentions, falling all over his handsome self to win his affections. Beth shrugged. "This whole thing was not my idea."

"Mine neither." He grinned at her surprise as he downed the mug of ale.

That didn't make much sense to her. "But ye are looking for a wife."

He shook his head, the wavy hairs that had escaped the leather tie holding the rest of his hair back hitting his strong cheeks, catching her attention, which annoyed her. "Nay, I dinna want one right now. The king decided to step in and control my life."

She scowled. "Mine as well."

He didn't want this? "At the Munro clan my da the laird is in charge. No one tells him what to do."

Ignoring her question, he waved at the server to refill his mug. "Do ye want more ale?"

"Aye."

He studied her. A little too carefully, she thought.

"Will ye be able to ride the horse back?" The twinkle in his eyes annoyed her.

She drew herself up and stared at him. "Aye. I can ride a horse after drinking several ales, and also when I am tired on a long journey. I can shoot an arrow dead on, and climb a tree to avoid a boar after drinking half a bottle of whisky, too."

His eyes grew wide. "It appears ye're trying to shock me."

She didn't answer but smiled. Let the arrogant oaf wonder.

He smiled back at her. "So ye are invincible?"

She laughed, and after a few moments of silence said, "Aye, I am invincible, and if we are talking here like friends over a mug of ale, let me tell ye I have no desire to marry. Not ye, not anyone. I like my life the way it is." She leaned forward and looked directly at him. "So, as yer friend, I suggest ye cast yer eyes in Lady Alice's direction."

He studied her for a minute, then said, "Nay. As lovely as Lady Alice is, I would ne'er consider her for a wife."

Rather than panic, she asked, "Why no'? She's pretty and quiet and her mam sure seems to expect ye to ask for her hand."

As she spoke, she tried not to notice his full lips and wavy red hair where it lay against the tanned skin on his forehead. His deep blue eyes staring at her caused flutters in her stomach as if a group of butterflies had arrived.

The laird's muscular body practically overflowed the chair and she found herself wondering how those large hands hugging the mug would feel running over her skin.

Not wanting to continue her thoughts along that line, she was grateful when he broke the tension, and said, "Because Lady Alice would ne'er be the right wife for me."

"Because?" She somehow knew there was an answer to that question and was just as sure she didn't want to hear it.

"And," he continued, as if she hadn't interrupted, "the only woman I would consider for a wife is ye." He grinned at her expression and lifted his mug of ale and finished the contents. "Are ye ready to return to the keep?"

CHAPTER FOUR

BETH'S MOUTH DRIED up and her heart began to pound. "I have no intention of marrying."

"So ye've said." He stood and threw a few coins on the table. "Come, lass, it grows dark and I ken yer parents will be worried."

Still stunned from his words, she merely followed him out of the inn and to the stables where he lifted her onto her horse, threw his leg over his own horse, and led the way, expecting her to trail behind him.

Which she did.

DANIEL HAD BREATHED a sigh of relief when he found Lady Beth in the village tavern inn. Relief was soon followed by a burst of anger, although he'd tried to hide it from her.

The lass apparently dinna understand how dangerous it was to travel by herself. Not that he was surprised, since in the very short time he'd known her, he expected her to do whatever it was that went against how other young lasses behaved.

This particular lass fascinated him. And even more so now.

After he had thrown a few coins on the table and escorted her from the inn, he placed his hand on her lower back, a true sign of possession. Which was a good thing to do in the village inn since he saw the way other men looked at her. Lady Beth might not belong to him yet, but if he had his way—which he generally did—she would be his.

Once they returned from the inn, he was greeted by Lady Chisholm staring pointedly at Lady Beth. "My laird, Lady Alice has been looking for ye. I believe ye offered to listen to her play the pianoforte this afternoon."

The perfect host, Daniel said, "I am verra sorry, my lady, but other things took up my time. I will be most happy to listen to her after supper."

Somewhat appeased, the woman smiled. "Thank ye, Laird, I ken Lady Alice was very disappointed when ye were no' here." She looked back and forth at him and Lady Beth as if she expected him to offer a further explanation.

He smiled at her. "Again I apologize, Lady Chrisholm, please offer my apologizes to Lady Alice and I will see you all at supper."

Lady Beth disappeared up the stairs right after Lady Chisholm cast her a look that said she was no more than a lightskirt.

Whistling a favorite tune, he ascended the stairs to his bed-chamber.

Let the battles begin.

BETH STUDIED THE dresses in her wardrobe, looking for the least attractive one to wear to supper. The atmosphere in the keep didn't necessarily lend itself to changing for supper like they were in some London fancy townhouse. However, Lady Chisholm had insisted that they should change for supper because it was the 'thing to do.'

A soft knock on her door drew her attention. "Aye."

Her mam entered the room, already dressed. "Where were ye all day?" She studied her daughter, looking as though she wished at times she and her husband had been more strict with their lass.

Beth shrugged. "Out riding, enjoying the fresh air."

She frowned. "Yer da and I were worried."

Beth pulled a dress from the wardrobe. "I ride by myself at home all the time." No, this dress would not do, it showed off more flesh than she wanted to present to the laird.

"Ye're no' at home now, and 'tis dangerous for ye to wander around by yerself. Yer da and I were so concerned we asked the laird to look for ye. Did ye see him?"

"Aye." This dress might be a good choice. She always thought the color was too dull for her coloring but had brought it along anyway. Yes, this was the perfect dress. She was sure Lady Alice would be dressed in a very fancy dress.

Her mam moved closer as if Beth couldn't hear her only five feet away. "Where did he find ye?"

She frowned, trying to remember the conversation they were having. "He dinna 'find' me because I wasna lost."

Mam's eyes narrowed. "Do no' disrespect me, lass. I am yer mam." She paused and continued, "then where did he see ye when ye weren't lost?"

Beth pulled the dress over her head to muffle her voice. "The village inn."

"What? I dinna hear ye."

She sighed. "At the village inn, I went there for an ale because I was thirsty and hungry." She turned to her mam. "They have an excellent meat pie."

Her mam sucked in a deep breath, ignoring the second part of her statement. "He found ye at the village *tavern* inn? Do ye ken how bad that looks for a young, unmarried woman to be alone in an inn? Was he angry?"

"Nay, he shared an ale with me."

Her mam stared at her for a few moments, then shook her head. "I will see ye downstairs in the great hall."

Beth knew she wasn't going to get away with anything strange about her appearance again, so even though she thought the dress unflattering, she still had to fix her hair in a normal manner. She cast a longing look at her brother's shoes and slipped on her own and left the room.

As she entered the great hall, Lady Chisholm was speaking with Laird Mackenzie, actually tugging on his sleeve as if that was the only way she could be sure he heard her. Beth walked past them and settled at the table on the dais between her mam and da. Daniel glanced over at her and smiled. She tossed her head and glowered back which only made the fool man laugh.

It appeared whatever she did, the laird thought it was funny. Hopefully that would change his mind about choosing her for his wife.

She suffered through supper with Lady Chisholm dominating the conversation, most of it about her daughter and her accomplishments and how large her dowry was. The lass kept her head down and ignored what her mam said.

It made Beth wonder why Lady Alice remained unmarried. She was a laird's daughter, had a generous dowry, and was pretty in her own way. Well, she didn't care what the lass's looks and manners were as long as Laird Mackenzie chose Lady Alice for his wife so Beth could return to her home and the life she found so pleasant.

Her mother's concerns rose unbidden to her mind, which she found more annoying than disconcerting.

Who will take care of ye in yer old age?

She had enough nieces and nephews to take care of her.

They'll be taking care of their own parents.

To shut off the voice in her head, she turned to her da. "How was yer day, Da?"

The words were no sooner out of her mouth than she realized he had been the one worried enough to ask Laird Mackenzie to find her. However, to her surprise, Da gave her a lengthy speech on how he'd spent a great deal of time in the morning speaking with the laird and his cousin and second-in-command, Gregory, learning many things about the castle, the Mackenzie clan, and some of the problems they were facing.

They'd also taken a ride around the area where the laird pointed out some things to him that his clan folk were doing that was very forward-thinking.

Then, he seemed to remember he'd had to ask the man to find her. "And 'twas worried yer mam was when she learned ye hadn't been back from yer ride, and was gone most of the day."

"I ken." Before he could ask her where the laird found her, she said, "It sounds as though the Mackenzie clan is doing verra well."

He agreed and continued to talk about all the things he saw. For her da to be so fascinated, the Mackenzie clan had to be impressive.

Once supper was finished, they all moved to another room where there was a piano forte, along with several other musical instruments. Since she hadn't spent too much time in the keep, she was surprised to see the room. "Do ye play instruments, Laird?" she asked.

Gregory snorted and after casting him a glare, Laird Daniel nodded, almost looking embarrassed in front of the men. "Aye. Even though I was to be laird of a powerful clan, my mam thought I should learn something else besides warrior training. She also made sure I could read, write and do numbers." He laughed. "My da did no' approve of the music part and he threatened me with a whipping if I told anyone. They fought about it all the time."

"It appears yer mam won the battle?" Her mam asked.

"Aye." He grinned. "But I must admit I haven't done much with it since she passed away four years ago."

Lady Chisholm perked up. "Well, Laird, ye doona have to concern yerself with music because my daughter plays the pianoforte perfectly."

"So you've said," Beth's mam muttered, but mostly everyone heard it.

Lady Chisholm sniffed and looked in her direction. "Do ye

play, Lady Beth, or do ye spend too much time on yer horse? My Alice doesn't consider horseback riding a very good use of a lass's time."

Her mam straightened her back in her chair. "My daughter plays just fine, Lady Chisholm," she said through gritted teeth.

Beth wanted to shut them all up and go to her bedchamber and read her new book, *Gulliver's Travels*, that she'd brought with her. Books were expensive and hard to come by, so she was very happy when her da had presented it to her before they left. She couldn't help but believe it had been a peace offering.

"Why doona we all sit down and let Lady Alice play for us?" Laird Mackenzie said with a certain amount of tension.

They took seats, and Lady Chisholm's words were true. Lady Alice played beautifully. Her face even lit up and she looked much prettier. Beth nudged Laird Mackenzie sitting next to her—too close, she noted—and lowered her voice. "See, if ye marry Lady Alice ye can both play music in the evenings."

He leaned even closer toward her. "When I marry, sweetheart, I have plans for my wife in the evening that doona include music. Except for the kind of music we make together." He had the nerve to wink at her.

She looked around to make sure no one saw him. Or heard him.

After about a half hour of playing, as Lady Alice was beginning to show the strain of performing, which led Beth to believe the poor lass was not used to showing off her skills to a group, Laird Mackenzie stood. "That was lovely, Lady Alice. Thank ye so much for sharing yer music skills with us."

The lass smiled and scurried from the instrument like a mouse escaping with a bit of a biscuit.

"Oh, but Laird Mackenzie, I was hoping ye and Lady Alice could play something together," Lady Chisholm said, actually tittering.

Beth was wiggling in her seat by then. She was not used to sitting still for so long. She groaned when her mam said, "We should have my daughter play now."

"Mam, I haven't played in a long time. I could ne'er play as good as Lady Alice." There. If Laird Mackenzie was hoping to have a musically-talented wife, even though he suggested another occupation for him and his wife in the evenings, she could be ruled out.

"Oh, no, Lady Beth. Ye must show us yer skills also." Lady Chisholm smirked and looked over at her husband who was softly snoring.

Mam nudged her. "Go play, Beth."

With a sigh she stepped up to the piano forte and sat. It had been months since she had the patience to sit and play music. She cleared her throat and decided that cracking her knuckles would send her mam over the edge. So she wiggled her fingers and then began to play the only piece she could do from memory.

Once she started to play and sing a very famous rather nasty tavern song, her mam stood, her face red. "I think I agree with ye, Beth, perhaps ye can practice while ye're here."

Beth stopped playing and looked over at Laird Mackenzie who was sitting next to Gregory. Both of them were doubled up with laughter. She would love to march over and knock their heads together. The arrogant oafs.

CHAPTER FIVE

DANIEL WAS SO sure of his choice of wife that he would have loved to invite Laird Munro into his solar right then and negotiate the betrothal agreement. Lady Beth was everything a young lass was not supposed to be. She rode a horse like a man, drank ale at the inn, also whisky if she was to be believed, and just now began to sing from memory one of the most popular tavern songs in Scotland.

But he knew if he pushed too hard too fast, she would find a way to completely step away. He needed to convince her, but he had to work at it. But then, anything worthwhile had to be won with hard work. He'd learned that as a warrior. If he hadn't had the training his da had insisted on, he would have been killed in one of the few battles in which he'd been involved.

Lady Beth made a quick exit from the room and he felt a tad let down since he'd intended to spend some time speaking with the lass and finding out what other outrageous things she was capable of.

THE NEXT MORNING Daniel headed to the stables just as Lady Beth was speaking with the stable master, her arms waving as she spoke.

"Is there a problem, lass?" he asked, knowing precisely what the issue was.

The lass turned to him, her hands on her hips. "Aye. Yer stablemaster said I couldna have a horse."

He shook his head, attempting to look regretful. "'Tis true, lass. I told him no' to let ye ride alone. As I said before, 'tis dangerous to be out there by yourself. Since ye are a guest in my home, 'tis my job to protect ye."

She growled. "From what?"

He smiled at that remark and took the reins of his horse from the stablemaster and said, "Yerself."

She scowled and he had to hold in his laughter. He'd given those instructions to his stablemaster because he wanted to make sure she couldn't leave without him. Despite the fact that he wanted to ride with her, it was truly dangerous for a woman to be outside the castle walls unprotected.

Even though times were quiet right now, the Jacobites were beginning to rattle their swords, which caused a lot of stress among the clans.

He'd heard recently that some clan folk were either tossed from their clans or left on their own because of a division in politics. These men roamed the area, attacking men for their coin and women for what they could get from them, whether they agreed or not.

"I am taking a ride now, so we can go together."

Instead of answering him, Lady Beth turned to the stablemaster. "May I have the same horse I had yesterday?"

She huffed when the man turned to him and looked for permission. "Aye, James, she can have the same horse. She had no trouble handling Tiger."

Once they were both mounted, Daniel led them from the outer bailey, across the drawbridge and off to the hills and valleys. They rode for about an hour before he shouted to her to follow him.

He led them to an area with a pond.

They both dismounted, guided their horses to the water and rubbed them down with grass. Again Daniel was impressed with how Lady Beth immediately began the procedure, not waiting for him to take care of her horse as most lasses would.

He decided it was time to take a chance.

Once she was finished with the horse, she turned to him, brushing her hands off. He stood only about a foot away and said nothing, only studied her. She looked up at him with confusion. Before she could say anything, he cupped her face in his hands and lowered his head.

Her lips were as sweet and soft as he'd thought they would be. So far she hadn't kicked him in uncomfortable places or bit his lips, so he took the kiss further, sliding his tongue along her lips until she opened. Warmth, sweetness, softness.

Tentatively, she touched her tongue to his. He pulled her closer, wrapping his arms around her plush body until he could feel her heart pounding against his chest. Unfortunately, she pushed him away and stood there, her breath coming in gasps. "Why did ye do that?"

Not sure himself since 'twas not planned he shrugged. "I doona ken. It just seemed like the thing to do."

She touched her lips with her fingertip. "I think we should return to the keep."

What he wanted to do was grab her again and kiss her until neither one of them could breathe, but he was certain this time he would get kicked or slapped in the face.

"Aye." He moved to her and hoisted her onto Tiger, then mounted Atlas, turning to lead them back to the open fields.

They rode slower than before, not speaking to each other, but at least she wasn't threatening to tell her da. Then again, she would not do that because he would demand they marry immediately.

After about another five minutes, he said, "Are ye all right, lass?" He couldn't stand the silence.

She stared straight ahead. "Aye."

He tried to think of something else to say, but couldn't, so he remained silent.

"Ye see that hedge up ahead?" She finally spoke to him, and everything seemed normal.

"Aye. I see it." He'd sailed over that shrub many times.

She looked at him with humor in her eyes. "Let's jump over it."

He shook his head. "I doona ken, lass. 'Tis an unfamiliar horse ye'er on, and that hedge is taller than it appears from here."

"Are ye afraid, then?" she said with a smirk.

"Nay, I've done it dozens of times but I doona think ye should do it." As soon as the words were out of his mouth, he realized he should not have said that. Lady Beth was not the type of lass to be told what to do.

Or what not to do.

She looked at him and grinned. He groaned when she kicked her horse's sides and raced toward the hedge. He followed but purposely stayed back so as not to distract her. He frowned, not liking the way she was approaching the hedge.

He held his breath as she sailed over the hedge cleanly and landed on the other side. She turned the horse and started back over again. He didn't think that was a good idea because the angle for the jump was off.

"Nay, doona try that!"

Either she didn't hear him or chose to ignore him. She flew over the hedge, lost her balance and went flying from the animal's back, landing in a heap, rolling a few feet before coming to a stop.

"Beth!!"

Chapter Six

HIS HEART IN his throat, Daniel jumped from his horse and ran to where Beth lay on the ground. He felt around her head first, but it didn't appear she'd had a head injury. Her ankle was bent and tucked underneath her leg. She was out cold.

He picked her up and strode to their horses. He shifted her around and smacked Tiger on his rump. Daniel knew he would return to the stable. He walked to Atlas and holding onto Beth, put his foot in the stirrup and swung his other leg over the horse, settling them both. He looked at her and she was still out.

He kicked Atlas's sides, and left for the castle. He rode as fast as he could, not wanting to tire his horse much more after their ride already. He breathed a sigh of relief when he spotted the castle.

Daniel rode into the outer bailey. "Get the healer and have her come to Lady Beth's bedchamber immediately!"

One of the guardsmen ran toward the small bothy set in the back of the keep where the healer lived. Daniel took the steps into the keep two at a time. When he entered the great hall, Laird and Lady Chisholm, Lady Alice and Laird and Lady Munro sat at the table, talking.

Lady Munro jumped up her eyes wide. "What has happened to Beth?"

Daniel continued toward the stairs to the bedchambers and

spoke over his shoulder. "She was thrown from her horse. The healer is on her way."

Lady Munro covered her mouth with her hand. "Oh my goodness." She moved quickly away from the table to join him.

"That's why my Alice doesn't ride. 'Tis verra dangerous, and not an appropriate thing for young lasses to do." Lady Chisholm had to get her opinion in. Ignoring the woman, Daniel continued upstairs.

Lady Munro arrived right behind him and opened the door to Beth's bedchamber. He carried her to the bed and gently laid her down. Her mam pushed the hair back from her face. She had a few scratches on her cheek, but no other visible injuries.

"What have we here?" The healer, Emma, hustled into the room.

"Lady Beth was riding and jumped over a hedge and was thrown from her horse."

Lady Munro laid her hand on her chest. Then she twisted her hands together and looked at the healer. "Will she be all right?"

Emma looked at Lady Munro. "Ye are her mam?"

"Aye."

"I need to remove her clothes so I can examine her." She looked at Daniel. "Ye will have to leave, my laird, and wait in the great hall. I will send word to you when I ken more."

He was reluctant to leave, but knew he could not stay in Beth's bedchamber, especially with Lady Munro undressing her, but he was truly worried about the lass. "Aye, but please do send word once ye've finished yer examination, or when Lady Beth awakens."

"I will, my Laird, now if ye would please leave so I can help the lass."

He nodded and turned to leave the room, feeling guilty for allowing Beth to take that second jump. Although with the lass's determination, he would not have been able to stop her, anyway.

BETH GROANED WITH the pain in her foot. She had no idea what was going on, but a woman she didn't know was slowly moving her fingers over her foot. "Ouch, that hurts."

"Where does it hurt, lassie?"

She whispered, thinking the less she used any part of her body the more it would make the pain ease. "My ankle."

The strange woman clucked. "Aye, that's what I thought."

Beth groaned. "Who are you and what happened? Why does my foot hurt so much?"

Her mam appeared at her bedside and took her hand. "Ye fell off your horse and it appears ye hurt yer ankle."

Beth frowned and spoke even though it hurt to even move her mouth. "I never fell off a horse in my whole life."

Her mam walked to the other side of the bed so the woman who was most likely a healer could continue to tend to her.

"Dear, according to the laird, ye were jumping and was thrown."

Beth closed her eyes and groaned. "I can just imagine what Laird Mackenzie will have to say about it."

"Actually, he was verra concerned about ye, and wanted a report once Emma examined ye," her mam said.

Her mam then proceeded to undress her as carefully as she could. When she was down to her last petticoat, the healer took over. As gently as she could, she ran her hands over her body. When she reached the foot that hurt so much, she placed her hand over her ankle and gently squeezed.

Beth jumped. "Ouch. That hurts." Her eyes filled with tears.

The healer looked at her with sympathy. "Tis sorry I am to hurt ye, Beth, but I had to be sure the bone wasn't broken."

Her mam took in a sharp breath. "Is it broken?"

"Nay. She just twisted it. The bone isna damaged. A few days of rest and hot and cold pads on her ankle will help."

Then she walked to the door and sent for a maid. "Tell the laird that Lady Beth is awake and appears to have a twisted ankle."

"What exactly does a twisted ankle mean?" Beth asked as she shifted and groaned with pain.

"It means when ye fell from the horse—"

Beth sucked in her breath and frowned. "I dinna fall."

"—ye twisted yer foot and I don't see any bad damage, but ye will need to keep yer weight off that ankle at least for a few days, maybe more. I will have one of the maids bring ye pads of cold cloths to place around yer ankle which might help with the discomfort. I can also mix ye a potion for the pain. Tomorrow ye can alternate between cold and hot cloths to help the muscle."

The maid the healer had sent to the laird to give him a report returned. "Emma, the laird is insisting he see Lady Beth."

Her mam looked at her with raised brows. "If the laird wants to see ye, we will have to dress ye again."

He probably wanted to laugh at her and comment on her bragging about being able to take a jump with no problem. She groaned again. "Can I just say nay?"

Emma and her mam both said at the same time, "Nay."

"He is the laird, Beth," her mam said.

She gave a very unladylike snort. "Oh aye, I almost forgot."

Meanwhile her mam was busy pulling out more comfortable clothes for her to wear and told the maid that Lady Beth would be ready to receive the laird in fifteen minutes.

"I'll put a couple of petticoats on ye with a bed jacket. With me here I am sure that would be fine. I think the less we move yer foot the better that would be." Emma nodded as Mam spoke.

By the time the laird arrived, mam had changed her clothes, washed her face and brushed her hair. The laird knocked softly and Emma called, "Enter."

Laird Mackenzie walked into the room with a frown on his handsome face. He looked at Emma. "The lass said Lady Beth twisted her ankle."

"Aye." The healer said, "There doesn't seemed to be any permanent damage to the foot, but she must have bedrest for a least a few days."

The laird walked over to her bed and smiled. Here it comes, she thought, him teasing her about the bragging she'd done regarding her skills on a horse. She sighed and looked up at him.

She was once more reminded how striking the man was. His muscles moved on their own as he entered the room. His wavy hair fell onto his forehead and with the way the strands stood up on end, it appeared he had been running his fingers through it.

Mam moved from her bedside to allow the laird to speak with her. "How are ye lass?"

She hesitated, waiting for the smirk he would give her to appear. "Well, my foot is twisted and painful, but my pride took a worse fall then the rest of me did."

The laird shook his head. "Nay. Ye did a beautiful jump, but when ye turned around, yer angle was off."

She shook her head, her eyes filling with tears. "Nay. I should have kenned better, but I was so interested in impressing ye that I dinna think it through."

He took her hand and lowered his voice. "Ye do impress me, Lady Beth."

She hated the fluttering in her stomach, but mostly she hated the look in her mam's eyes. Just what she needed, to give her mother more encouragement.

Laird Mackenzie turned to the healer. "Must she remain in bed, or can I carry her downstairs?"

Beth sucked in her breath. The last thing she needed was The Mackenzie traipsing all over the keep with her in his arms. Lady Chisholm would have apoplexy and Da would ask the laird to get together to work out the betrothal agreement.

"Aye, Laird, she doona have to remain in bed, just as long as she doona try to walk," Emma said.

A bright smile lit the laird's face. "That is good news. I will carry her downstairs so she can break her fast."

Beth shook her head, her panic mounting. Things were getting out of hand. Laird Mackenzie was assuming too much. She had to stop this. "Nay. I can have a tray brought up."

"Let the laird help ye, Beth," her mam said with a look in her eyes that terrified her.

Before she could protest again, he had scooped her up and was heading toward the door.

She wiggled, trying to get out of his arms, almost throwing herself to the ground. "Ye doona have to do this, ye ken."

He tightened his grip, telling her with his strong arms that he had no intention of letting her go. "Ye are my guest, I cannot have ye stuck in yer bedchamber."

Full scale panic surging through her, she said, "Yer guests are going to get the wrong impression. Lady Chrisholm for example."

The laird scowled. "*Pssh*. The lady drives me crazy. 'Tis my keep, and I am laird. If I wish to carry an injured guest, I shall do so."

They arrived in the great hall just as food was being brought out. Since the warriors were already gone, it must have been the second serving. Lady and Laird Chisholm, along with Lady Alice, were chatting away in their seats when Laird Mackenzie and Beth entered the room.

"What is this!" Lady Chisholm rose halfway from her seat, her face red and eyes wide.

"As I told ye before, Lady Beth had an accident this morning," Laird Mackenzie said. "She canno' walk for a few days."

Lady Chisholm raised her pointed chin. "Then the careless lass should remain in her bedchamber, instead of parading all around the keep in her bedclothes."

Beth could feel the muscles in his arms tighten. "Lady Beth is no' in her bedclothes, and it 'twould be verra boring for her to lay in her bed. She is my guest, and therefore, my responsibility." Before she could say anything else, he turned to her mam. "Mayhap once I place yer daughter in her seat, ye may help to get her settled."

Taking her place again, Lady Chisholm sniffed. "That's what comes from lasses no' behaving like ladies and running around on horses and getting injured. My Alice rarely rides a horse, 'tis verra unladylike." She wasn't done. "And I find it verra improper for the laird to be carrying a young lass around the keep in her bedclothes, guest or no'."

※※※

DANIEL HAD NEVER wanted to toss a guest from his house more than he did Lady Chisholm. Even if he had been interested enough in Lady Alice to take her as his wife, the thought of having that woman as his mother-in-law would stop him cold.

Lady Munro glared at Lady Chisholm. "I doona think ye need to worry about my daughter, Lady Chisholm. She is a lady in all the ways that matter."

Daniel stifled his laughter but gave Lady Munro a wink. She smiled back.

He put Beth in a seat as far from Lady Chisholm as possible. Her mam immediately settled her in. He took the seat next to her.

"Ye ken this doesna look good?" Beth said, her voice lowered.

He spoke softly as well. "Ye care what Lady Chisholm says?"

"Nay, but I doona trust the woman. She's determined to push Lady Alice off on ye, and as much as I doona wish to be considered for yer choice I doona think having Lady Chisholm in yer life would be good."

He grinned. "Well. 'Twould be easy to keep her out of my life."

HE LOVED WATCHING her squirm. "Are ye no' going to ask me why?" he urged.

She shook her head, her cheeks turning red.

He lowered his voice. "I think ye ken."

She ignored his statement, but shifted in her seat.

Lady Chisholm stared at them; her eyes narrowed.

Daniel had chosen to ignore the woman. He turned to Lady Beth. "Are ye uncomfortable? I can move ye to one of the chairs in front of the hearth and get a pillow for ye to sit on."

"Nay."

He glanced at Lady Chisholm who looked as though she was ready to stab Lady Beth with her eating knife.

"I doona want to call any more attention to myself," she whispered to him, making furtive glances at the woman. He was just about finished with his meal when Lady Chisholm leaned forward and looked down the dais. "My Laird, since ye seem to be in charge of ill guests, Lady Alice is feeling a tad lightheaded. Will ye please take her for a walk in the garden so she can get some fresh air?"

He groaned under his breath, but as a good host, he stood. "Of course, I would be pleased to take Lady Alice to the garden."

Lady Alice looked uncomfortable as he approached her. He got the impression the lass didn't want him as much as he didn't want her. Either that or she was extremely shy, which was even worse. He would never want a wife who blushed every time he spoke to her.

But the only way he was going to get rid of her—and her mother—would be to have Beth accept him. He could have the betrothal agreement done with her da already here at the castle, plan the wedding, say their vows, then drag her luscious body into his bed.

He couldn't wait to run his hands over those very tempting curves, which he'd been admiring since she'd arrived and had the pleasure of feeling as he'd carried her.

The silence between him and Lady Alice as they strolled was growing uncomfortable. Finally he cleared his throat. "What are yer favorite activities, Lady Alice?"

She spoke to her shoes. "I am well-trained in running a keep, I can play the pianoforte. I can sew and deal with servants."

Her words came out stilted as if she'd been taught to memorize them. There was no doubt in his mind who had pounded the words into her head.

Not exactly what he'd asked, however. "Do ye like to read?"

She shook her head. "Nay. I ne'er learned."

How would she be expected to run a keep if she never learned to read? He tried another way. "Do ye like to play chess?"

"I ne'er learned how to play chess. My mam says 'tis no' good for a lass to learn. She says it taxes the brain too much."

He was growing desperate and decided if he was to get rid of Lady Alice he had to convince Beth to marry him. Were he not interested in her either, he would just go to the elders and tell them to notify the king that neither woman would be a good wife for him, and get his privacy back.

But he wanted Beth. He was determined to have her and cursed the fact that the one woman he wanted didn't want marriage, and the one he didn't want had a mother who was pushing her daughter at him.

He could probably seduce Beth since he'd never had trouble with the lasses lifting their skirts for him, but a forced marriage because he'd compromised her was not something he wanted for her. She would despise him for the rest of their lives.

After another ten or fifteen minutes with neither of them speaking, he led Lady Alice back to the keep.

She seemed relieved.

As was he.

CHAPTER SEVEN

ETH HAD BEEN amused when Lady Chisholm had asked the laird to walk Alice around the garden. Instead of looking "a tad lightheaded" the lass looked like the last thing in the world she wanted to do was take a walk with The Mackenzie.

Thinking about their time here, Beth had begun to realize that based on her behavior, Lady Alice was no more interested in being chosen for the bride than she was. It was most likely her mam who wanted her daughter to marry the laird. Poor Mackenzie. The king had presented him with two women to choose from who apparently didn't wanted to be selected.

How very odd when one thought about it. A young handsome Clan Chief of a very powerful clan, and from what she'd seen, wealthy, with a caring way about him, and yet these two women were not interested in being chosen as his wife.

Once she'd started to tick off all Laird Daniel Mackenzie had to offer, she'd begun to feel foolish herself. Why was she so against marriage to this man when he had so much appeal?

Who will take care of ye in yer old age?

One of the young maids from the kitchen arrived at her side holding a wet cloth. "My lady, the laird asked the kitchen to replace the cold cloth ye have with a new one every half hour or so."

"Well, thank ye verra much. The healer said it would help the swelling from my injury."

The young lass smiled, dipped slightly and headed back to the kitchen.

"Ah, I see my orders are being followed." The Mackenzie had walked up to her when she'd been speaking with the maid.

Beth turned and the flutters in her stomach that always occurred with the laird awakened with force. Yes, he was handsome. Yes, he had a warrior's body that made her wonder what it would feel like for him to wrap those powerful arms around her, so much so that she had a hard time looking at him for long. Especially with the look in his blue eyes that had begun to darken.

"Are no' yer orders always followed? Is that also a requirement for a wife?" She knew her voice was strained due to the dryness that had arrived with the fluttering.

The humor in his eyes disappeared and he leaned in. "Are ye seeking the position, lass? 'Tis available, ye ken. But only to ye."

She gulped and knew her cheeks were cherry red. To help eliminate the prickly feeling she'd had since he'd walked up, she shrugged. "Nay, but I think we have already discussed that."

He pulled the chair across from her closer, sat down, and lowered his voice so only she could hear him. "Aye, but just so ye ken, I doona consider the discussion over."

Why when he was near, did she have this loss of her senses? Her words got tangled up and she had a propensity to say things she should not allow out of her mouth.

However, she was still determined not to marry.

"Here ye both are. My Alice was looking for ye." Lady Chisholm walked in to stand in front of them, her hands resting on her stomach, a downcast Lady Alice alongside her.

Beth hid her giggle as Daniel softly growled. "So nice to see ye and yer daughter, Lady Chisholm."

"Lady Alice was looking forward to a walk in the garden, Laird." She glanced at Beth. "'Tis sorry I am that Lady Beth is unavailable, so 'twill only be the two of ye."

"One more walk in the garden and I will hang myself from the nearest tree," the laird said under his breath.

SUPPER WAS FINISHED and Beth was feeling restless. All day sitting in a chair had strained her body as well as her brain. She normally had a very busy schedule when at home. However, most of the day she had been entertained watching Lady Chisholm chase The Mackenzie around the keep, dragging her daughter behind her.

He had been gone for the last couple of hours and had mentioned to her after he settled her back in her chair after the noon meal that he was going to spend time at the lists.

Now Mackenzie walked up to her with Lady Chisholm and Lady Alice following him like a mam duck with her ducklings lined up behind her.

"How good to see ye, My Laird." She acted as though she hadn't seen him in days. "And good evening, Lady Chisholm, Lady Alice. I hope ye had a pleasant day."

"My daughter was just mentioning how nice it would be to take a tour of the castle. She hasn't seen more than the keep in the time we've been here."

Mackenzie offered the woman a strained smile and said, "I will definitely give Lady Alice a tour, however, I had just asked Lady Beth if she would like to play a game of chess." He looked over at Lady Alice who was again examining her shoes. "Ye are more than welcome to join us."

Instead of the young lady answering, Lady Chisholm frowned. "My Alice doesna ken how to play chess. It strains a women's brain and is no' something a lass should do."

Her eyes narrowed in concentration. "If ye would play chess in yer lovely music room, my daughter can entertain ye with music."

"Nay," both Beth and Mackenzie said at the same time.

Beth did her best to smile at the woman who was as irritating as a bee buzzing around one's face. "I am sorry, my lady, but I would find it verra distracting for such a focused game."

Lady Chisholm sniffed and said, "Sounds as though ye aren't that good of a player if some lovely music would distract ye." When Beth offered no retort, the woman sighed. "Verra well, my daughter will be happy to observe ye."

Beth glanced at Lady Alice, who looked as she always did, uninterested and withdrawn.

The four of them left the great hall, Mackenzie carrying her, Lady Chisholm grumbling all the way about how a young lady who was injured should be in her bed, not being shuffled around the keep like a bag of flour.

Once they were settled in the laird's solar, Mackenzie and her facing each other over the chess board, he said, "Do ye play chess, lass? I ne'er asked if ye could."

"Aye. I play a bit." There was no reason to say it had been years since anyone beat her at the game. She decided to have a bit of fun with him because she was bored and could use the entertainment. 'Twas also a way to deflate that huge ego he strutted around with.

The game started out slowly, with Beth deliberately making poor choices. It was great fun figuring out how to appear incompetent while not making moves that would reveal her expertise to the man. She felt a flush of success when Mackenzie tried to play tutor and mentioned the things she was doing wrong, and how to improve on her bad moves. She nodded and continued to make mistakes, holding in her laughter.

After suffering through a few more games, Mackenzie said, "I think that's enough for the night. Ye seem a bit tired."

Now was the time to have her fun. "I think, with yer help tonight, I learned a lot. Can we play one more game?"

'Twas obvious he wasn't interested, but being a gentleman and their host, he agreed.

Makenzie set the board back up.

"What say ye we have a wager?" Beth asked, trying very hard not to smile.

In her corner, Lady Chisholm huffed and muttered something about inappropriate young women placing bets with men.

"Ach, lass, I doona believe ye improved that much. I would feel like I'm cheating ye. What kind of wager did ye have in mind?"

She tapped her chin, as if giving it a great deal of thought, even though she'd known from when Mackenzie first asked about a chess game that she wanted another trip to the village. "If I win, ye will take me to the village for a second visit so I can see something else besides these walls."

He offered her a warm smile. "Even if ye doona win, I will take ye on a trip to the village."

"Oh, what a wonderful idea!" Lady Chisholm emerged from her snit, her smile bright, her hand grasping Lady Alice's arm firmly, as if afraid the lass would run off. "Lady Alice would love a trip to the village, wouldn't ye, dear?"

Apparently growing tired of her mam's constant pushing her, Lady Alice nodded, but her lips were firm.

The laird looked at Beth over the chess board. "And if I win, I will…" Glancing at Lady Chisholm, he said, "think about what I want."

They both bent over the board and within four moves, Beth slapped her knight down in front of the king and announced, "Checkmate!"

Mackenzie just stared at her, his jaw slack. "What…what…what just happened?"

Beth sat back and laughed. "I think it's apparent, Laird Mackenzie, I just checkmated ye."

He shook his head in confusion. "But the game just started."

She continued to grin. "Aye, and now 'tis ended."

Lady Chrisholm waved her hand at the chessboard. "'Tis time to end this, anyway. Watching ye play is quite boring for poor Lady Alice."

Beth was angry enough to remind Lady Chisholm that she had not been invited to sit and watch them play, but conversations with her mam about good manners kept her from commenting.

Mackenzie continued to stare at her. "How many other things are ye hiding, Lady Beth?" His grin told her he wasn't just referring to expertise at chess, but the costume she'd worn the first day as well as her comfort sitting in the tavern inn, and jumping over a hedge.

"Lady Alice doesna have any secrets, do ye daughter?" Lady Chisholm nudged her daughter in the side and the poor girl flushed red from the top of her dress to her hairline.

After a few moments of awkward silence, Mackenzie slapped his thighs and stood. "I guess ye've gained another trip to the village, Lady Beth."

"What time shall we be ready, Laird?" Again that annoying voice that Beth had begun to hear in her dreams. Or nightmares.

"I'm afraid we need to wait a few more days, my lady. Lady Beth is no' ready to walk around. The healer would have to give her permission."

"Oh, but Lady Alice doesna have an injury. We could go tomorrow."

Daniel took a deep breath. "Lady Chisholm, ye remember, of course, that a visit to the village was what Lady Beth chose for her win. I doona think 'tis the thing to do that we go and leave her behind."

Beth didn't think she could take any more of Lady Chisholm. Manners or not, she was about ready to yank the hair from the woman's head.

And shove it into her always-open mouth.

DANIEL CARRIED BETH up the steps to the bedchamber floor. "I asked one of the maids to have tea sent up. I have a jug of whisky arriving as well. I think after all that time with Lady Chisholm, I need more than tea."

He pushed the door open and carried her into the room.

"I doona think 'tis proper for ye to send for refreshments to be brought to my room. 'Twill no' look good."

He nodded. "I agree. Why doona I send a message to yer mam to join us? She would certainly be enough of a chaperone for even Lady Chisholm." He placed her in the chair by the fireplace.

Beth shifted around, looking uncomfortable. "I doona think ye have to worry about Lady Chisholm finding us together. The last thing she wants is for her daughter to be eliminated due to ye compromising me doing something inappropriate."

He smirked. "I wouldn't mind her finding us together doing something inappropriate."

Then he shook his head and raised his hand. "Nay, I doona want ye to be forced into something ye seem to be against." He smiled at her. "Unless ye've changed yer mind?"

Before she could answer his question, a knock on the door drew their attention as the maid arrived with a tray of tea and sweet pasties. Right behind her was a lad with the jug of whisky.

Daniel took the jug from the lad's hands. "Giles, can ye please go to Lady Munro's bedchamber and ask her to come to her daughter's bedchamber?"

Before Beth had set up her tea the way she liked it, Lady Munro burst through the door. "Are ye well, Beth? Did ye hurt yer ankle again? I kenned ye shouldn't be wandering all over the keep."

"Mam, I'm fine. The laird and I are having refreshments, and we needed a chaperone."

Beth's mam put her hand to her chest. "Oh, goodness." She took the chair next to Beth. "I could use a cup of tea myself."

They talked about the chess game and Lady Munro laughed when Daniel complained about Beth pretending she didn't know how to play and then checking him in four moves.

"Aye, my daughter has stunned us for years with her ability to play the game. Also, no man can do numbers better than my daughter. Give her any sort of mathematical problem and she'll do it in her head."

Like a proud mam, she continued "She loves to read, and has read all the books we have. No' to brag, but Lady Beth is skilled in many areas, but I'm afraid few of them are the typical ladylike endeavors. She plays chess—as ye found out. She rides horses well—unless she doesn't try too many jumps." She smiled at her daughter, then she took a sip of her tea.

"Add to her list that she has helped deliver several lambs, but much to her da's dismay she canno' sew, run a kitchen, or dance in a graceful way."

By the time Lady Munro finished, Daniel was laughing. The more he saw and the more he heard, he was determined to have this woman for his wife. He imagined their uncommon life.

He had to start wooing the lass. He'd been letting her keep a distance between them, but he kenned it was time to put an end to that.

His only concern was Lady Alice. Her mam made sure they both popped up everywhere, so he and Beth have had very little, if any, time alone. That was what he needed.

He, Lady Munro and Beth chatted for a while and Daniel realized that Lady Munro herself was a very nice woman, intelligent and charming, especially as she told stories of her numerous grandchildren. According to her, those bairns were perfect.

He looked at Beth when her mam went on and on about them. She rolled her eyes a few times which made him wonder if her opinion varied from her mam's.

Eventually, Lady Munro began to fidget in her seat and looked at him. "I think 'tis time I retired. That bit of whisky ye gave me did its work to make me drowsy." She stood and said, "Ye will need to leave us now, Laird. I must prepare my daughter for bed."

He climbed to his feet and nodded. "Aye, my lady." He turned to Beth. "Good sleep to ye."

He left with the full intention of returning once Lady Munro left the room. There was something he needed to say to her and the time was now.

He heard the door to Beth's room close and waited until he heard Lady Munro's as well, then walked down the corridor and knocked lightly before easing it open.

She was in bed, her coverlet to her waist, which she immediately drew to her chin, her eyes wide. "What are ye doing here?"

"May I come in for a minute?"

She hesitated for a moment, then nodded. He walked into the room, closing the door behind him. Beth wrapped her arms around her middle and stared at him. "I doona understand. 'Tis no' proper for ye to be here. If anyone finds out, there will be trouble."

"I doona want to cause ye problems, and I willna take much of yer time."

He drew up a chair and sat alongside her, resting his foot on his opposite knee. He ran his fingers through his hair and cleared his throat. "I have hinted at this, but the time has come for me to state it clearly. I want ye for my wife, Beth. I think we suit and could have a good life together. I have plenty of money, and a strong castle to defend ye. I will ne'er hurt ye and will give ye plenty of bairns to fuss o'er."

She narrowed her eyes. "Ye just said the wrong thing. I ne'er wanted lots of bairns."

So his suspicions about her reaction to her mother's obvious fondness for her grandchildren hadn't been wrong. He grinned. "I plan to spend plenty of time making them, so we will be sure ye have help to care for them."

"I dinna say *aye*." She drew up her knees and rested her chin on them. "Ye ken I dinna want to come here for the purpose of presenting myself as a broodmare." When he began to speak, she raised her hand. "I wish I could say I've changed my mind, but I'm torn."

She sucked in her breath when he climbed on the bed and sat next to her. He wrapped his arms around her warm soft body. "At least ye dinna say nay." When she began to shake her head, he placed his finger on her lips.

Then he cupped her face in his hands and covered her lips with his. A slight, innocent kiss turned into something more, something needy, powerful, and passionate.

Before he did more than he should—certainly not more than he wanted—he leaned back and kissed her on her forehead. "I will see ye in the morn. Please think about what I said."

CHAPTER EIGHT

FIVE DAYS LATER, Beth rose from her bed after a poor night's sleep. Despite the passing of time, Daniel's proposal still troubled her. He didn't hesitate in his offer of marriage, but was it considered a true offer? Had he left her that night and then spoken with her da? Surely her da would not begin a betrothal agreement without her consent? And surely he would have told her if negotiations were taking place.

She'd been resting and now her foot was feeling much better. Daniel had been busy with clan problems for most of the last few days. Evenings were spent with them together, along with Laird and Lady Chisholm, Beth's parents and, of course, Lady Alice. She'd grown to know Daniel so well that she sensed when he was annoyed with Lady Chisholm and her insistence that Lady Alice be included in everything.

Since Lady Alice was an invited guest, it was only proper that they include her, but she didn't want to do anything they suggested. One could only take so many walks in the garden.

Beth had enlisted her mam in an effort to take Lady Chisholm off their hands so she and Daniel could do something—anything—without Lady Chisholm's constant chatter, since wherever Lady Alice went, so did her mam.

After a few days of entertaining the woman, Mam was just as disgusted with Lady Chisholm as they were. "And the poor lass doesn't seem to be interested in anything," her mam said one afternoon about Lady Alice as they took tea and time alone in her parents' bedchamber to relax their ears.

"With her mam disapproving of everything, 'tis no wonder she has no interests beyond sewing and music."

All those thoughts muddled her mind while she was dressing for dinner. She loved her life at Foulis Castle. In fact, she had never questioned her happiness. Not until she met Daniel Mackenzie and he made her start thinking about everything she'd imagined she wanted in her life.

As he had pointed out, he was young, wealthy, Clan Chief of a powerful clan, and in charge of a well-protected castle. And, he said, he would give her many bairns. She smiled to herself. That was one point against him.

What he hadn't needed to point out was he was one of the most handsome men she'd ever seen, with those classic nobility features, curly, deep red hair and his blue eyes full of merriment and, at times, passion. She'd learned about that with the few kisses they'd been able to share while Mam was busy with Lady Chisholm.

Kisses that made her body tingle and turned her into a mass of jelly with no way to keep herself standing up if Daniel hadn't been holding her tightly against his strong chest with his strong arms.

She took one last glance in the looking glass and again tested her ankle, which seemed to be just fine.

"I doona see why we must wait for her. We are wasting time." Lady Chisholm's grating voice met her as Beth entered the great hall.

"Lady Chisholm, as I've pointed out to ye before, 'twas Lady Beth who requested this trip to the village. 'Twould be quite ill-mannered to leave without her."

"Well ye can see my Alice is here and ready to go," she huffed. "If ye be choosing a wife, ye want one ye are no' always waiting on."

Apparently not having seen her yet, Lady Chisholm continued, "'Tis bad enough we've had to wait all these days because of her foolish injury. My Alice and I are quite tired of watching the two of ye play chess."

Daniel sighed. "I've told ye before, my lady, ye are welcome to use one of our carriages to make a trip to the village yerselves. I am most certain Lady Munro would be happy to travel with ye."

Daniel looked over at her as she arrived at the dais and smiled. "Good morn, Lady Beth. Ye are looking lovely this day."

Lady Chisholm turned, most likely annoyed that Beth had appeared. She sniffed. "Some women should not wear that particular color."

Since Beth was quite sure the woman did not refer to her own daughter, it appeared the insults were going to start before they even left the castle.

"Good morn to ye, Lady Chisholm, Lady Alice." She dipped before she took the seat Daniel held out for her.

"We were thinking perhaps ye were ill and unable to go with us on our trip," Lady Chisholm said, not exactly kindly.

Daniel shook his head in frustration. "If Lady Beth was unable to go, we would put our trip off because, as I've said many times, 'twas her request after winning the game of chess that I take her to the village."

No one else might have noticed the tension in Daniel's voice, but she knew him well enough to realize his temper was growing. Not wishing to cause any further trouble, she sat and reached for some fruit, cold meat, and a mushroom pastie.

"What is the best thing to see in the village, my laird?" Lady Chisholm asked. The woman actually fluttered her eyelashes, and Beth almost choked on her piece of meat.

"There are many things to see in the village, Lady Chisholm. There is a baker's shop, an ironworker, a glass blower, a stone mason, and on certain days—like today—crafters and vendors from all over the Highlands with fancy things for women and food items for sale."

"Oh, how exciting!" Lady Chisholm clapped her hands. While Beth was looking forward to a day out of the castle since she'd been confined due to her injury, Alice looked, if anything, bored. Beth had no idea what the lass's problem was, but it was easy for anyone to see that she did not want to be at Castle Leod, did not hope to be picked as a wife for laird Daniel Mackenzie, and all she seemed to be concerned about was leaving.

The carriage ride was nice, with Daniel pointing out various bothies and farms. Many of the farmers and their families waved at them as they passed.

Lady Chisholm pulled her skirts closer to her body as if just the sight of the people would dirty her. "I doona understand why ye are so friendly with these people," she said, sniffing.

"They are my people, Lady Chisholm. They are members of Clan Mackenzie and therefore, my responsibility."

She raised her chin. "It seems to me if they dinna have so many bairns, they wouldn't be yer responsibility. I ken my Alice would no' allow herself to have too many bairns. They tire a woman out and take away any time she might have for herself."

DANIEL WAS SO tired of Lady Chisholm that he wasn't sure he could take another day with her. Mayhap he could claim to have an ague, but he refused to hide in his own house and had too many duties to see to and people who were counting on him.

He glanced over at Beth, and he swore either she was asleep or doing a good job of faking it. 'Twas something he would consider doing, but they were almost at the village, and he didn't want to end up running into a tree.

"My laird, I heard from yer chatelaine that there is to be a gathering of the clan members in another week's time."

"Aye, tis Beltane, We celebrate it every year."

According to the king's edict, he was to be married—or at

least betrothed—by Beltane. He was certain the elders were expecting him to have a betrothal agreement in hand by then.

Despite the requirement hanging over his head, he had no intention of doing so unless he'd received an aye from Beth. If the event was in another week, he had better apply more pressure on the lass without pushing her. Otherwise, he would defy the elders and the king himself, state he had decided on no one and then travel to Foulis Castle to continue pursuing Beth.

Let the king do what he must. 'Twas his life.

He glanced over at Lady Alice and was once again struck by her total disinterest in just about everything she had done during this much too long visit. It was apparent that her mam was the one interested in this match.

He could not remember the last time Castle Leod hosted any sort of party. When he was growing up, his da had spent most of his time in Inverness and London, and his mam suffered from "nerves" so she rarely left her room.

Like Lady Alice?

Left to his own devices, the lonely child spent a great deal of time outdoors, doing the usual things lads do, and when he grew older, his da arrived home at one point and introduced him to his tutor.

Mr. Gage worked with Daniel for years, teaching him all the things his da should have been doing. One time when Daniel asked Da why he was never home, he merely stated that he could not stand his wife's company.

He couldn't help wondering if his mam was another Lady Chisholm. He'd never seen her much, spending most of his time with his tutor and other lads in the area doing all the things young lads do.

When they arrived at the village, he jumped down from the carriage and turned to assist the ladies. Due to recent rains, the ground was wet, but Beth had smartly worn boots, whereas Lady Alice and her mam had on slippers better suited to the gathering they were so looking forward to. Of course, that forced them to hang onto his arms. When he glanced over at Beth she grinned, apparently knowing his thoughts about the predicament he was in.

Instead of enjoying the day alone with Beth and moving ahead with his pursuit of the lass, he was stuck with these two on his arms, with Lady Chisholm's voice screeching into his ear every minute. Did the woman ever breathe?

"My laird, Lady Alice and I must go somewhere we can dry off our slippers. 'Tis getting quite cold with them wet."

He watched Beth, wearing sensible half-boots, wander from the three of them and begin looking at a vendor selling small animals carved from wood.

Daniel walked them all over to where Beth was browsing, picking up little animals from a woodcutter's table and studying them. "I think this would be just perfect for my nephews."

"How many nephews do ye have?" Daniel asked.

"Six."

Lady Chisholm tsked. "Ye ne'er have to worry about Lady Alice imposing that many bairns on ye, My Laird."

Beth turned to the woman. "My nieces and nephews are from two different mothers."

Ignoring her comment, Lady Chisholm tugged on Daniel's arm. "I can feel Lady Alice shaking. We must get to a place where we can warm ourselves and dry out our shoes."

Since there was no way Lady Chisholm could feel her daughter shaking since they were on different sides of his body, he chose to ignore correcting her on that. "Aye. 'Tis sorry I am. I will take ye to the village tavern. 'Tis small, but they have a few tables there and a braiser that will warm ye."

He nodded to Beth. "I will be back once I get the ladies settled."

Lady Chisholm sucked in a breath. "Surely ye doona intend to leave me and my daughter alone in a village tavern?"

Beth attempted to hide her smile as Daniel squeezed the bridge of his nose with his index finger and thumb. "My lady, ye will be fine. I ken the owner of the tavern and he will watch o'er ye. I *did* promise to spend time with Lady Beth on this trip, so please be patient and allow us some time to look around the village as I promised."

Lady Chisholm began to protest, but Daniel walked, pulled, and dragged them to the tavern. He introduced them to the owner, Gabriel Mackenzie, and told him to give them whatever drink or food they wished, and that he would return in a couple of hours.

Before he could get caught up in another demand or complaint from Lady Chisholm, he hurried from the tavern and strode up to Beth.

Her grin turned into laughter as he approached her. "Did ye get yer guests all settled in the tavern?"

"I am finding it harder all the time to no' dump her into the nearest loch." He took Beth's arm. "If Laird Chisholm wishes to marry off Lady Alice, he best do whatever negotiations necessary without his wife present, or even within shouting distance." He shook his head. "I have ne'er met anyone like that woman. I noticed Laird Chisholm has been mostly hiding in his room or out and about with yer da since they arrived, and now I ken why. Were she my wife, I would be standing in front of the judge, explaining where I had buried the body."

He picked up one of the small wooden animals and looked it over. "These are quite nice. This mon is verra talented."

Beth nodded. "Aye. I think I am going to purchase one for each of my six nephews. Then I must find something suitable for my nieces."

He found he was enjoying learning about Beth's family. He had known from speaking with Lady Munro that there were several grandchildren. However, once he'd gotten her on the subject, it was hard to speak of anything else.

"And how many nieces do ye have?"

Beth smiled, obviously enjoying talking about the little ones. So she wasn't against bairns, just not her own. He needed to discover if she was afraid of giving birth, or having the responsibility. But then, knowing her as he did so far, she didn't seem to be afraid of much.

"Just two, but my sister, Patricia is expecting her first and she swears it's a lass."

"Do yer sisters and their families e'er get together all at the same time with yer mam?"

Beth rolled her eyes. "Oh, aye. Almost every time one of them comes, 'tis like the others have ways to read each others' minds because they all show up at the same time. 'Tis chaotic."

He couldn't help laughing. As an only child, he could not imagine what it would be like to have a keep full of bairns. "I am sure yer mam loves that."

"Aye. She is crazy enough to love the confusion."

"And ye donna?"

Her face softened. "I love my nieces and nephews, and I even love when they all come at the same time. But I am also glad when they leave." She looked up at Daniel. "Ye see, when they are yer own, they doona leave."

He laughed again. "'Tis true, but I'm no' sure ye want yer own bairns to leave. And, as I told ye, there would be plenty of help should we marry and have lots of little ones."

Beth looked off into the distance and he couldn't help but wonder if she was re-thinking her position on marriage. He certainly hoped so. He was anxious to call this visit with the lasses over and move on to important things. Like marriage.

And the bedding.

After purchasing the six little wooden animals, they continued to browse; most of the vendors were familiar with him and enjoyed teasing him about the bonny lass by his side.

Beth was not immune to their comments, because she spent a lot of time with reddened cheeks.

They moved onto another vendor he didn't know, where Beth bought two pretty ribbons for her nieces.

"Are ye hungry lass?"

She glanced at him sideways with a smirk. "Mayhap, but it depends on where ye put Lady Chisholm and Lady Alice."

He stopped and placed his hands on his hips. "They are at the tavern. Lady Chisholm was no' happy about where I brought her, but there was no other place."

"And Lady Alice?"

He shrugged. "As usual she dinna seem to care where she was."

Beth tucked the wooden animals and ribbons into a small sack she carried with her, then took Daniel's arm and they continued to walk. "I believe there is something wrong with that lass."

"Aye. I do as well."

They began to pass the tavern. Lady Chisholm emerged and waved her handkerchief at them. "Oh, Laird Mackenzie, Lady Alice and I are ready to leave. I'm afraid our shoes are still wet and we are certain to catch a chill."

Daniel groaned. "'Tis sorry I am, Beth, that this trip wasna what ye hoped for." He moved her toward the screeching woman. "'Twas certainly no' what I had hoped for."

CHAPTER NINE

D ANIEL SAT IN his solar, tapping his fingers on the desk, staring at the three elders, anxious to get the unexpected meeting over with. He knew what they sought to hear from him, and he was certain what he planned to tell them. However, since he hadn't received the answer he wanted from Beth, he had no intention of responding to their questions.

Deciding to turn the meeting against them, rather than put himself through questions for which he yet had no answer, he said, "I heard from Lady Chisholm that a gathering, or party, or whate'er ye wish to call it to celebrate Beltane has been planned." He stared all three of them in the eye and continued, "I am still the laird, and I make the decisions. 'Twas bad enough ye allowed the invite to two young ladies and their parents without my knowledge."

Abraham waved him off. "'Twas the king's edict. Ye might be the laird, but as yer advisors, 'tis our job to see that the king's order is carried out."

Daniel's anger grew. "What does that mean? I can dismiss all of ye at any time. The only reason I have no' as of yet is out of respect for my da. But I've been laird for years and no longer need yer advice. Or interference."

Richard leaned forward. "Aye. Ye no' longer need our advice, but ye would remain unmarried for another ten years if we dinna push ye."

Daniel narrowed his eyes. *Push him? Did they reach out to the king for him to be pushed?* "Did ye have anything to do with the king's order that was delivered?"

Their denial was anything but forceful, but he didn't have the desire to investigate it right now. "Again, if I chose to marry tomorrow or in another ten years, 'tis no' something you need to place yerselves into." He crossed his arms over his chest, ready to end this "meeting" as soon as possible. He had more important things to do than soothe the egos of the elder advisors whom, he had a strong suspicion, had overstepped themselves this time.

"From what we've seen ye seem smitten with the Munro lass," Morgan, the youngest of the elders, well in his sixth decade, grinned at him.

Daniel glowered back at the three of them. "What happens between Lady Beth and Lady Alice and myself is no' up for discussion."

Abraham smirked. "Just bed one of them and then the decision would be made."

Blood pounding in his head, Daniel growled. "That is no' only a bad suggestion, but casts dishonor on both lasses' reputations. I do no' wish to obtain a wife who feels obligated into it. I will make a decision, and I when I do, ye will be informed. I doona plan to be rushed into such an important matter."

Morgan narrowed his eyes at Daniel. "Lady Chisholm seems quite eager to have ye decide on Lady Alice."

If he didn't call an end to this discussion, he would say something that he would later regret. Or make the grave mistake of punching one of the old men in the face.

He had depended on these men for guidance when his da had first died but he hadn't felt the need in a long time. "I repeat, whatever is happening between me and the lasses is no' up for discussion."

Abraham turned toward Richard. "From what I've seen, tying

himself with Lady Alice and having to deal with her mam would make for a difficult life."

Morgan nodded. "Then Lady Beth it is." He sat back, grinning like a fool, as if it were his decision to make.

Daniel slapped his thighs and stood. "I am calling an end to this so-called meeting. Any further interference from ye will result in me banning the three of ye from the keep." He left the room to the sound of Morgan's voice, but didn't stay long enough to hear what he said.

He had no intention of listening to anything else from the men. If things were going the way he wanted, he would already be working out a betrothal agreement with Laird Munro. But his stubborn daughter needed more persuasion, which he planned to do, facing the one-week deadline imposed by Beltane.

He left the keep to visit a few tenants who were having concerns and wanted to discuss them with their laird. With guests at the castle, and an event planned he wasn't too fond of, he did not have the time to set up a clan court anytime soon.

When he stepped into the stable, his attention was immediately drawn by a familiar voice, causing him to smile. Beth was speaking with James about a horse to ride since, based on what he'd heard, Tiger had suffered an injury.

"I think the lady can handle Bessie," Daniel said as he moved next to Beth. He ran his hand over the mare's back. "Doona let her name fool ye, lass," he said at Beth's raised eyebrows. "She is a strong horse who is easy to handle and will give ye a good ride."

He glanced at her foot. "Is yer ankle well enough to ride?"

She moved it back and forth, gently, he noticed. "Aye. As long as I doona ride for too long. 'Tis still a tad tender after yesterday's trip to the village."

The strong feelings he had toward the lass rose again as he studied her beautiful face, mesmerizing blue eyes, and her wealth of blond hair pulled back in a heavy braid that hung down her back.

"Are ye headed anywhere in particular?" he asked as he accepted his horse from James.

"Nay. I thought to just ride and get some fresh air."

"Just a reminder, lass, I doona want ye riding away from the castle without an escort." He assisted her into the saddle and placed his hand on Bessie's back running his hand over her smooth hide. "I have to visit with a few clan members who have been having some issues that need to be dealt with. I could probably use some of yer advice as I listen to their tales."

Beth perked up. "Aye, I would like that. I helped my da several times when he held clan court."

Daniel shook his head. "I am no' surprised, I can see ye whispering in yer da's ear."

Beth let out with a burst of laughter. "Nay. I dinna do any whispering. I stated my opinion—when my da asked for it—and he generally agreed with me. 'Twas almost as if he was preparing me for clan leader."

It hadn't occurred to him that Beth might be out of reach if she was destined to be Munro Clan Chief since some clans were set up to pass to a female. "Preparing for clan leader? Is that why yer da let ye go so long without arranging a marriage for ye?"

"Nay. I doona inherit when my da passes. Since my parents had all girls, the Clan Chief position goes to my cousin, Nathan, my da's brother's oldest son. I think da just enjoyed watching me tease my mam by doing another thing not considered proper for a lass."

He laughed at the panic that had at first gripped him, realizing if she had been in line for the clan chief position, she would have said so before now because that would have been a perfect excuse for her not wanting to marry. He also chided himself because her parents would not have consented to this visit if she was slated for such a future.

He swung his leg over his horse. "Are ye ready?"

"Aye."

"If yer ankle starts to trouble ye, let me know and we will stop."

BETH NODDED AND followed Daniel as he rode away from the castle and in a different direction than where they'd gone before when they visited the village.

The air was cool and crisp. Even though the Highlands never got hot, the summer, which was growing closer, made the air very comfortable. The scant sun warmed her further as they traveled over hills and small valleys. She had no idea how vast the Mackenzie clan lands were. She knew like most large clans, there were a number of various castles within the Mackenzie clan, each having its own chieftain, with Daniel being the Clan Chief.

Daniel slowed his horse down and waved to her right. "We take that path through the woods."

Beth nodded, turned her horse and followed Daniel. There was a definite path through the wooded area, but not wide enough for them to ride side by side. Their positions gave her an excellent view of Daniel's strong warrior body. His tight buttocks, bulging thighs, and massive shoulders made her feel small. And very strange.

She had wanted to continue with their kiss the other night but was somewhat grateful when he backed up and left her room. She was finding the man much too attractive and didn't think she would have stopped him had he not had the common sense to do so.

Within minutes it seemed, they broke free of the woods and faced five bothies in a circle.

Each one had a garden of flowers in the front with vegetables and what appeared to be herbs in the back. Several bairns ran around the space, chasing each other and a few puppies.

Acres of land stretched beyond the bothies with sheep wandering about with sheep dogs and a few men keeping them from leaving the flock.

"Laird, how good of ye to visit us." A plump, cheerful looking woman came out of one of the bothies, wiping her hands on a well-used apron.

Daniel jumped from his horse and then helped Beth down. She stumbled a bit when her ankle gave her a sharp pain.

"Are ye all right, lass?" Daniel asked as he grabbed her around her waist.

"Aye. My first time riding since the injury, and I'm afraid 'tis a tad stiff."

Still supporting her, he walked her over to where the woman stood. "Mrs. Sarah Mackenzie, may I present Lady Beth Munro, a guest at Castle Leod."

A man came around from the back of the house. He stuck his dirty hand out and Daniel took it with no problem. A true laird.

The man looked like the perfect husband to the woman. He was large, with hands as big as gloves, patched trousers, and a sturdy work shirt. A cap covered his head, and his smile was very engaging. "Good to see ye my laird. Do ye have a minute to look over a patch of land I had an idea for, just a mile or so?"

"Aye." He turned to Beth. I think ye'd be better off here with yer ankle still troubling ye."

"Are ye no' well, Lady Beth?" Sarah said, looking concerned.

"I hurt my ankle last week and 'tis still a tad sore."

The woman reached out for her and took her arm. "Come inside, lass, and I'll fix ye some tea. I have lovely teacakes I made this morning and if I wait too long, this group," she motioned with her head to the bairns, "will eat them all. And I have a salve the healer gave me for my husband's sore muscles that might help ye."

Feeling welcomed, which felt familiar from visits with her own clan members, she wondered what Mrs. Mackenzie thought of her being with the laird. Too polite to ask, of course, she could imagine what ideas were going through the woman's mind.

The inside of the bothy was just as well-kept as the outside gardens. The furnishings were worn but clean. The house smelled of biscuits and the dishes piled in the sink were a testimony to the baking the woman had done.

A woven basket filled with clothes sat on the kitchen floor. In all, the bothy looked like a warm, welcoming place with everyone well-fed, and two caring parents for the little ones.

There had been times when she had visited her own clan members' homes, that she would wonder what her life would have been like if she hadn't been born into a laird's family. While she and her parents worked hard in their keep, they had servants to do the heavy chores, they had more room than those who lived in the bothies, and most likely more of the better food.

She knew her sisters had plenty of help with their children. When the bairns had their tea and biscuits, there were maids to help with the messes the little ones made.

There were also maids to help with bathing and dressing the children. That was all the things she would have if she married Daniel.

So why was she holding out to continue her life as it was with no changes, no differences, no husband, no bairns?

Who will take care of ye in yer old age?

She did as much as she could to avoid too close contact with her nieces and nephews when her sisters visited, mainly because she never liked the look in her mam's eyes when she watched her with the bairns.

But what if she had one of her own?

Nay.

She and Mrs. Mackenzie spent more than an hour speaking of all things that women seemed to be able to share and talk about regardless of their station in life or ages.

At one point during their conversation, Beth looked down at the bairn with big brown eyes staring up at her. At some point, she had climbed into her lap. She had crumbs from a biscuit mixed with drool sliding down her chin.

Instead of the normal uneasiness she would have felt had it been one of her sisters' bairns, she actually drew the warm, soft little body closer.

Until she began to wail. Then she handed the mite back to her mam without qualms.

The two men arrived back just as Mrs. Mackenzie was rounding the little ones up for a nap, the crying one tucked firmly against her hip.

She smiled at Beth. "Doona fash yerself about little Asa. She always cries when 'tis time for her nap."

Still feeling uneasy, she joined Daniel as he and Mr. Mackenzie shook hands. A bit stiff from sitting all that time, he had to again help her onto her horse. Once settled, they left the area.

"Did ye and Mrs. Mackenzie have a nice visit?" Daniel asked as they rode away from the bothy.

"Aye." She shook her head. "She is a charming woman and does a wonderful job of taking care of all those bairns."

Daniel gave her a strange look. "It looked like a lot of work to ye?"

Beth shrugged. "Nay. Mrs. Mackenzie had it all in hand."

He smiled, apparently encouraged by her response. "How many bairns were there?"

She had to think for a minute. "Four."

Then they entered the path through the woods and there was no more conversation.

⇶⫸⫷⇷

THE MACKENZIES, MUNROS, and Chisholms had just begun to eat their supper, with Lady Chisholm once again holding court in her usual annoying voice, when a man raced into the great hall, looking frantically around. "Where is the laird?"

Daniel stood. "Aye, Malcolm, what is the problem, lad?"

The lad looked frantically around. "My wife is having bad pains, and I doona ken what to do."

Daniel walked around the dais and approached the man, putting his hand on his shoulder. "Calm down, lad. Is it close to her time?"

Malcolm ran his fingers through his hair. "I think so. Maybe no'. No' sure." He twisted his cap in his hands and looked as if he was about to cry.

"Where is the healer?" Daniel asked.

"I doona ken." His voice cracked. "I went to her bothy but she wasna there."

One of the serving maids who carried in a platter of food said, "Emma is off to visit her sister. She said no one was due to give birth for another three weeks."

Poor Malcolm grew even paler and looked as though he was going to faint. "Three weeks? Gertie is having pains now." He looked toward the dais where the women sat. "Can her pains last three weeks?"

Beth left the table and walked up alongside him. "I can help ye, just take a couple of deep breaths."

Despite the serious situation, Daniel could not help but smirk at the lass. "I am sure ye can help."

Beth immediately took over. She grabbed one of the passing maids and said, "Go to Emma's bothy and gather as many linens as ye can." Next she looked over at Daniel. "Have the horses readied."

Lady Chisholm stood, aghast. "Ye are an unmarried lass, Lady Beth. Ye cannot possibly go near a woman giving birth. 'Tis no' allowed."

Lady Munro also stood. "I will go with ye. I assisted at many of my grandchildren's births, plus I had a few of my own." She rounded the table and joined the maid. She turned back to Beth. "I will help the young maid gather the necessary medicants for the lass."

Malcolm appeared a combination of relieved and confused. He didn't seem to know where to go or what to do. Daniel took him in hand. "Come with me to the stable, lad. We will ready the horses so they will be available when the women join us."

Lady Chisholm was not to be quieted. "My Laird, I canno'

believe ye are allowing yer guests to get involved in the birthing of a bairn. Especially to one of the farmers. 'Tis unheard of."

Lady Munro had already left the great hall with the maid, their two heads together. Daniel, Malcolm, and Beth made a quick exit from the keep to the sound of Lady Chisholm's bellowing and fanning herself, insisting she was about to faint. Daniel sincerely hoped so; he was ready to knock the vile woman unconscious himself.

As he looked back, he saw that Lady Alice continued to sit still, studying her trencher of food.

CHAPTER TEN

BETH HAD NEVER delivered a human baby, but she'd assisted in plenty of animal births in the stables at home. She'd thought about asking her da to join them since he'd also helped with many parturitions, but her mam gasped in horror when she suggested it.

"Ye canno' have a man help deliver a strange woman's bairn, Beth. Whatever is wrong with ye? They doona even allow the husband to be there."

"I was just thinking about all the animals Da had participated in birthing."

"Beth! He would need to look between this woman's legs!" Mam was so discombobulated, she blurted that out without thinking she was speaking to her unmarried daughter. But then again, her unmarried daughter was, herself, going to view the birth of a baby and her mam suddenly seemed to realize it.

"Now that I think about it, ye shouldna be here either. Unmarried lasses are no' allowed to see this."

Beth raised her brows. "I was there for Patrick's birth when we were visiting Alisa's keep."

"Aye, something I would have chased ye from but yer sister insisted ye stay there to hold her hand." Her mam was still breathing deeply, and Beth, feeling soundly chastised, remained quiet for the rest of the ride, realizing that yes, birthing a human was certainly different from birthing an animal.

They arrived at the bothy right behind the Mackenzie, who had summoned them. She really must learn these people's first names since everyone she'd met so far had been a Mackenzie.

Why do you need to know if you're going home?

The screams coming from the window drew Beth and her mam to the poor woman's home. As they walked towards the door, Daniel wrapped his arm around the husband's shoulders and moved him off. "Come, I brought some whisky with me."

The man stopped in his tracks and shook his head. "Nay. I doona want to be too far from Gertie."

Just then another loud bellow came from the bothy. Malcolm winced and looked over at Daniel. "I think maybe a bit of liquid might be just the thing right now."

Beth grinned as he turned and hurried away, Daniel on his heels.

HOURS LATER, BETH and her mam walked from the front door of the bothy and wiped the sweat from their foreheads. Gertie, whose name Beth had found out during their long session was resting peacefully, along with the healthy lad she'd delivered.

Right after Beth and her mam had arrived, the three bairns the new mother already had were taken home by Gertie's sister. Then two neighbors came to help as well as another of Gertie's sisters.

With all the women present, Beth and her mam really weren't needed, but the others seemed to look toward her mother for guidance, most likely because she was an older woman and told the group she had birthed four bairns herself with no problems.

In all, it had been an easy birth for the mother in spite of all the screaming. It was interesting to once again witness a baby being born. While not terribly different from an animal's birthing, there was something about watching the small infant as soon as he'd slid from his mam's body that moved something in Beth's mind and body.

Her mam looked at her as she held the slippery, screaming infant in her hands, making a point of mentioning the joy of it all several times.

Beth watched the smiling new mam reach out for the bairn once her mam had washed the tiny body, snugly wrapped it, and handed it to her.

The look of love and amazement on Gertie's face, even though she had already birthed a few other children, brought tears to Beth's eyes and a lump to her throat.

THE SUN WAS just making its appearance when Daniel and the new da stumbled up the path to the bothy, their arms around each other, singing a Scottish tune. It was hard to tell who was supporting who.

"How is Gertie?" Malcolm slurred.

At least that was what Beth thought the man said. He had obviously lessened *his* pain. She glanced over at Daniel and he looked almost as bad as Malcolm.

Malcolm stumbled past Daniel, Beth and her mam. "I must see my wife."

Daniel swayed on his feet. "He will probably pass out. When he awakens in the morn, he can see the new...?" A bleary-eyed Daniel looked at her questionably.

"Lad."

"Now, sweetheart, doona look at me that way. Malcolm will suffer for sure once he wakes up."

Aware of the look that her mam passed between them at how Daniel had addressed her, Beth grew uncomfortable. Before Daniel could say anything else to encourage her mam, Beth grabbed his arm and walked off.

"I will see ye at the keep. I feel a tad exhausted," her mam said, still smiling as she climbed on her horse.

Beth glared at Daniel, her hands on her hips. "How do ye intend to get home? Ye canno' ride yer horse."

The laird drew himself up. "I am perfectly capable of riding Atlas." He stabbed himself in the chest with his thumb. "I am a warrior. And laird." He leaned in and grabbed her shoulder to keep from stumbling.

Beth sighed and shook her head. "Ye will have to ride with me. Otherwise, ye will end up on yer foolish head."

Daniel grinned. "Ride with ye?"

She walked off and brought her horse to where Daniel stood, leaning against a tree looking as though he would fall asleep right there.

"I will slap my horse and we can both ride Atlas since he is the bigger horse."

"Aye. Like me," Daniel said.

Ignoring him, she gave the horse she had ridden a slap on her rump, knowing she would return to the stables.

"Can ye mount up?" She was trying hard not to smile since she did not want Daniel to think she approved of how he had kept Malcolm occupied.

She had to admit she was pleasantly surprised at how agile the laird was in getting onto the horse, although for a minute she thought he was going to slip off the other side.

He turned to her and grinned. "Yer turn."

Since her mam had asked one of Gertie's sisters to send the dirty linens from the birth to the castle, Beth was free-handed.

Daniel put his hand out and pulled her up in front of him. The strength of his arm amazed her. He settled her on his lap, then wrapped his arms around her, pulling her close. They started off on their return to the castle with Daniel nibbling on her ear.

She elbowed his chest. "Stop that."

"Does it make ye feel good?"

"Nay."

She could feel him grin behind her. "I doona think ye are telling the truth, sweetheart."

"Stop calling me that. I am no' yer sweetheart." Truthfully, the term did warm her. She ne'er thought to hear those words from a man since she'd always eschewed marriage.

"Ye could be my sweetheart." He began nuzzling her again. "What say ye join me in my bedchamber when we get back to the castle."

Beth sighed. "Nay. I will no' join ye in yer bedchamber. 'Tis no' proper."

He pulled her closer while she tried to concentrate on keeping Atlas from wandering off the path to graze, or worse, to roll them off.

Once again he began kissing her neck, then his hand wandered up her body, cupping her breast. She sucked in a breath, about to push his hand away, when he pinched her nipple and she jumped. It felt strange. But good.

"Daniel, ye should no' be doing this." Her voice sounded strange to her.

"Shh, sweetheart. Just relax and enjoy it."

His hand moved up to the top of her dress and he slid his finger in, circling her nipple. The kisses on her neck grew more intense and she was certain he sucked the skin under her ear.

She had to stop him; they were coming close to the castle. With the sun rising, the guardsmen were changing and they would give the men a wonderful sight to talk about for a while.

She pushed at his hand, pulling it from her bodice. "Daniel, ye must stop."

"Nay, love, I would do this for the rest of yer life." He fumbled again, trying to put his finger back.

Beth shook her head and swatted at his hand. "I dinna say 'aye' to yer proposal, Daniel."

"Ye will."

Just then they reached the lowered drawbridge which told

her the men had seen them coming. Hopefully no one had eyesight good enough to see them from a distance.

Once they reached the outer bailey, one of the stablemasters helped her off the horse, and then Daniel all but slid onto the ground.

"Yer laird has had a busy night. I need one of the men to put him to bed." She didn't mention the busyness he'd had was helping the new da to get through his wife's birthing by getting them both drunk.

Daniel reached out and grasped her forearm. "Nay, lass, I want ye to put me to bed."

Beth could feel her face begin to flush. She shook his hand off and grabbed his shoulder as he began to fall. She turned to Gregory, who was grinning like a fool. "Please take yer laird upstairs."

Gregory threw his arm over Daniel's shoulders and moved him forward. "Let us go to bed, Daniel."

He stumbled as he tried to turn around to look at her. "Is Beth coming? 'Tis no' ye I want to go to bed with."

"Nay, Laird. Lady Beth is finding her own bed."

As they walked off, she heard Daniel say. "She can have my bed. With me."

Beth took a deep breath and headed to the stairs. She pondered whether she should break her fast first before going to her chamber. Realizing she probably wouldn't be able to sleep if she was hungry, she hurried upstairs so she could clean up before she ate.

Her mam was coming down the stairs as she was going up. "Is the laird well?" she asked.

"Aye," Beth said. "Gregory is bringing—probably dragging—him to his bedchamber."

Her mam smiled. "He seems to have a fancy for ye, daughter."

She shook her head and closed her eyes. "Please. Doona ask."

✴⟫⟫✕⟪⟪

DANIEL AWOKE TO gloaming. There was a fire in the brasier in his bedchamber, which someone must have started. He was still dressed and his head felt as though someone had slammed the flat side of a sword on it.

His mouth was as dry as a virgin's cunt. He sat up and held his head, trying to remember if he'd had a good enough time to make up for the pain.

He stumbled to the door and shouted, "Jesse!" He immediately regretted yelling like that and almost brought up whatever was left in his stomach as the pain in his head increased.

The lad from the kitchen rushed into his room a few minutes later, panting. "Aye, my laird. What is it?"

"Lower yer voice, lad." His own sounded like a frog had taken up residence there.

"What is it laird?" Jesse whispered.

"Get me as much ale as ye can carry. Then send Gregory in here."

Jesse nodded and left, walking on the tips of his feet.

Gregory knocked, then entered his bedchamber a few minutes later, a grin on his face. "How are ye feeling, my laird?"

"Like *shite*." He moved to sit on the bed. "I think I remember coming home this morning on Atlas. Was Lady Beth with me?"

It was obvious Gregory was attempting to hold in laughter. "Aye, she was, and wasna too happy with the way ye kept touching her and suggesting she join ye in yer bed."

"*Devil's bones*, so it was as I remember? Was she mad e'ough to leave for home?"

"Nay. She dinna seem upset. More like she was embarrassed and verra tired."

Jesse raced into the room, and handed Daniel a jug of ale which he gulped down, feeling a tad better. He held the jug back to the lad. "More."

Daniel turned to Gregory. "What is the time?"

"About an hour past supper. I think it would do you well to have something to eat."

"I need to clean up and then I will be down. I'd like to speak with ye after I eat."

Gregory nodded and Jesse returned with another jug of ale, the poor lad completely out of breath. "Thank ye, lad. This will help a lot."

Once he cleaned up, changed clothes and began to feel like a human again, Daniel headed for the great hall.

Beth was nowhere in sight, but, unfortunately, Lady Chisholm was still seated at the dais, almost as if she waited for him. "There ye are, laird. Lady Alice has been looking for ye all day."

He doubted very much if the lass had been looking for him, but he merely nodded. On the other hand, he was quite sure Lady Chisholm had been waiting for him to appear. "How can I help ye, Lady Chisholm?"

He took his seat and one of the serving maids brought him a trencher full of wonderful smelling stew with a loaf of warm bread, butter, and a chunk of cheese.

Lady Chisholm moved from her seat to the one next to him. "Lord Chisholm has been wondering if ye need to speak with him before the Beltane festival."

The woman's push had gone from amusing, to uncomfortable, to downright annoying. "Nay. I dinna need to speak with yer husband."

Her lips pursed and she glared at him. "I just wanted to give ye a chance now rather than leaving it to the last minute."

When he continued to eat and ignored her, she leaned in close and said, "We all ken that Lady Beth is no' suited to be yer wife. She doesna have the necessary ladylike manner about her and she seems a bit loose with her favors." She nodded as if imparting a secret.

Daniel placed his eating knife carefully on the table. He didn't want to have to explain to the elders why he'd committed murder. "Lady Chisholm, there is nothing wrong with Lady Beth's manners and if ye dare to repeat what ye just said about her favors, which is completely untrue, I will personally put ye out of the castle in a verra uncomfortable manner."

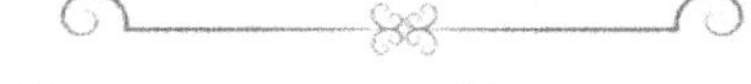

CHAPTER ELEVEN

THE PREPARATIONS FOR Beltane had been going on for what seemed like days. Beth had been forced to put up with Lady Chisholm during all the planning, decorating, and deciding on the food to be served, almost as if she was Lady of the Manor.

Louise, the chatelaine, had given up, literally throwing her hands in the air when Lady Chisholm interfered once too many times.

Beth and Daniel had been spending time together, mostly playing chess in the evenings. He had been out most of the days tending to problems with his clan. Although, she thought, he was merely avoiding Lady Chisholm.

Despite the interfering, annoying woman's best efforts, Daniel had been able to get some time alone with Beth. His kisses left her breathless, and he'd taken a few more privileges that she should not have allowed, but she had a way of forgetting herself when he kissed her.

He was still trying so hard to get an "aye" from her. Although she never said so to him, she was getting close. There was no reason for her to continue to eschew marriage. She knew by now that she loved the arrogant oaf and even though Daniel had never said the words to her, she was almost certain he felt the same.

He'd mentioned more than once that the advisors wanted him to make a betrothal announcement at the festival. She hadn't asked him what he would do if she hadn't given him the answer he wanted by then.

She knew he had no intention of accepting Lady Alice despite the lass's mother's constant barrage of comments on her daughter's skills, good manners, virtuous demeanor, and ability to run a keep.

In all the time they'd been there, and despite Beth's best efforts, she was unable to speak much with Lady Alice. Her mam was always by her side, almost as if she was guarding her. Could she be that concerned about the lass's virtue?

How easily the woman had taken over the job of Lady of the Manor, making it obvious she fully expected Daniel to accept Lady Alice.

Beltane always included the entire village with a huge bonfire in the village green. Beth had thought it unnecessary to decorate the castle so much, but no one had the courage to go against Lady Chisholm's dictates.

"I doona understand that woman," Beth's mam said as, arms linked, they strolled in the garden, mainly to get away from Lady Chisholm and the way she ordered everyone about.

"I ken ye and the laird have become friendly," she glanced at her with a smirk, "so unless I am completely fooled, I doona think the laird plans to marry Lady Alice."

"I can tell ye one thing for certain, Mam. Daniel does no' wish to marry Lady Alice. And anyone with eyes can see they do no' have an attraction to each other."

"She doesna like anything he likes, she doesna talk to him, and doesna even look him in the eye. If there was ever a lass who let it be known she has no interest in a mon more than Lady Alice, I'd like to meet her."

They continued to enjoy their walk, admiring the new spring flowers in full bloom and the warm air. Hopefully the weather would continue to cooperate that evening when the bonfire would be held after supper.

After a few minutes, her mam said, "Is there something between ye and the laird yer da and I should ken about?"

Beth glanced sideways at her mam and said, "Mayhap."

Her mam burst out with laughter. "Mayhap?"

Beth grinned. "Aye. Mayhap."

"'Tis obvious to yer da and me, as well as others in the keep, that the laird has a fancy for ye."

Now it was Beth's turn to laugh. "A fancy?"

Before she could comment on that, Lady Chisholm stood at the front of the garden and hustled toward them. "Oh, Lady Munro. We need yer help in here, if ye and Lady Beth are finished with yer walk."

Beth sighed and muttered, "I swear the woman follows me. No matter where I am, she turns up. I expect to find her in my bed one night."

Her mam mumbled, but Beth heard her say, "That better be the only one yer da finds in yer bed."

They joined the woman and Beth, still reeling from Mam's comment, decided to head to her bedchamber.

"Oh, Lady Beth. We would so much like yer opinion on some of the decorations. Lady Alice did so much of the work, but now 'tis yer turn." Lady Chisholm waved her finger at her, a smirk on her face.

She wished there was someone here who had the daring to shove the woman onto her bottom. In the nearest loch.

"Aye. I would love to help," Beth said as she glanced at her mam.

Beltane always included the entire village with a huge bonfire in the village green. Beth had thought it unnecessary to decorate the castle so much, but no one had the courage to go against Lady Chisholm's dictates.

THE BELTANE FESTIVAL was in full swing. The weather had

cooperated and the night was clear and chilly, but the bonfire kept everyone warm enough. Along with the whisky and dancing.

Daniel and Beth stood side-by-side watching the antics of the revelers. Older men who should be seeking their beds were still jumping up and down to the music. Highlanders loved a party.

"Do ye think ye can do another dance?" Daniel asked her as he took a sip of his ale.

"I doona ken. I'm a tad warn out from all the dancing." She shook her head and pointed to an older man twirling a young girl around. "I doona ken how they do it."

Daniel grinned. "Fergus does it because he kens he will lay in his bed for the next three days, having his sons do all the necessary chores."

Before she could respond, they heard the familiar, annoying voice. "Oh, there ye are Laird." Lady Chisholm walked up behind them, dragging Lady Alice. "Lady Alice was hoping ye would dance with her."

She shoved the poor girl, who stumbled and landed in Daniel's arms. He quickly straightened her and backed up a few steps. Beth had to hide her grin at how quickly he got rid of her.

Being the gracious host and laird, he looked at the lass. "Lady Alice, would ye like to dance?"

She nodded, looking at her shoes. Her mam gave her another shove and this time Daniel caught her by the arms and they made their way to where the dancers were hopping, jumping, and twirling around the bonfire.

"Donna they make a great couple?" Lady Chisholm said as Daniel and Alice joined the dancers.

Refusing to give the answer the woman wanted, Beth merely shrugged.

"My Alice has everything the laird could possibly want in a wife." Lady Chisholm placed her hands at her middle and sighed as she watched them.

Beth had to use all her good training to keep quiet at a conversation she had no intention of having with this woman.

"If ye will excuse me, I need to make a visit to the garde-robe."

Lady Chisholm reached out and grabbed her arm. Rather forcefully. "Doona plan on marrying the laird, lass. My Alice will be his wife."

Beth pulled her arm free and walked off without comment. The woman was not only delusional, but frightening.

DANIEL WATCHED THE brief conversation between Beth and Lady Chisholm, and then Beth's quick departure. He didn't have to think too hard to imagine what that was all about. He really had to get Beth to give him the answer he wanted so he could make his announcement and be done with the annoying and pushy Lady Chisholm.

Although the crowd was loud, Lady Alice made no effort to speak with him. He tried a few times, but was only rewarded with a nod or shrug.

Thankfully, the bagpipes, fiddlers, and flutists decided to take a break and he was able to walk Lady Alice back to her mam. Without changing his pace, he turned on his heel and headed to the keep to find Beth. He found her sitting on one of the stone benches in the inner bailey when he arrived. "Are ye hiding from Lady Chisholm, too?" he said as he joined her.

"Aye."

"The musicians are taking a break, but I asked them to play something slow so I can take ye in my arms."

"Is that so?" she said with a smirk. "Suppose another mon has already asked me to dance a slow one?"

He leaned in close to her ear. "I will make sure the dance with ye is the last thing he does."

Beth laughed, that tinkling sound he loved so much. He stood and took her hand. "Come, Old Noah is no' kenned for taking long breaks."

They rounded the castle walls, heading to the bonfire when Lady Chisholm walked up. "Laird. I'm so glad to see ye. They say the next dance will be a slow one and Lady Alice is so looking forward to a slow dance with ye."

He nodded. "I am sure there is a lad who will be happy to dance with her, but I promised this one to Lady Beth."

Lady Chisholm huffed and walked away.

Daniel took a deep breath. "I doona ken how much longer I can tolerate the woman."

The music started up and Daniel swung Beth around and took her in his arms.

Perfect.

She fit him exactly right, just like in all the other ways. Their hearts beat as one, as they should. He tugged her closer and she laughed. But she didn't pull back.

After five or more minutes, the music ended. He took her by the hand and led her away from the bonfire.

"Where are we going?"

He smiled at her. "Somewhere private. I need time with ye, lass."

"I'm no' sure this is a good idea."

He shook his head and placed his finger over her lips. "Just for a few minutes. Things are simply too loud at the bonfire."

After a few minutes, they were in a small glen with which he was very familiar. Even in the dark, the star-studded sky and bright moon highlighted the area. Dips and valleys in the distance gave the space a feeling of being on top of the world.

He turned and gathered Beth into his arms. He lowered his head and took her mouth in a searing kiss. No hesitation on her part, she responded with fervor. He pulled her close enough that they were plastered against each other.

He wrapped his arms around her waist and she slid her hands up his chest and encircled his neck. The feel of her soft body against his almost drove him crazy. He wanted her so much. Definitely in his bed, but also in his life. She was perfect for him. He was growing nervous about Lady Chisholm and had to get a definite answer from Beth so he could see her father, and get the wedding date set.

No matter what it took, he would not lose her.

BETH HAD LOST all reason. Daniel's lips, warm skin, muscular chest pressed against her breasts brought strange feelings to her stomach. And lower parts.

He pulled away and began to nibble on her ear, leaving kisses in the trail of his mouth as he moved from one ear to the next, nibbling on her skin. "Ach, lass, ye're driving me crazy."

His hand slowly made its way down her shoulder to her breast, where he pinched the nipple begging for his touch. She gasped, and he covered her entire breast with his large warm hand, kneading, plucking, and bringing even more pleasurable feelings to her body.

"This is what we can do all the time if ye agree to marry me, sweetheart. There are so many ways I can bring ye pleasure, so many ways we can pleasure each other." He moved his mouth to her ear. "Say 'aye'."

She tried to shake her head no, but he gripped her bottom and lifted her until she felt what she knew was his male part, which was very swollen.

No longer remembering what she was saying 'nay' to, she groaned and rubbed back and forth. Daniel sucked in a breath and moved his head to her neck, scattering kisses, nipping, sucking.

He pulled back and she slowly opened her eyes. "Say 'aye', lass."

His eyes were black, his entire face tense with passion. Why was she saying nay? A lifetime of this kind of activity, of enjoying

Daniel's company, beating him at chess, and one day bearing a bairn who looked like a combination of him and her.

It might not be so bad having a bairn or two. It might even be fun.

Before she could answer, he said, "What can I do to get an 'aye' from ye, sweetheart?"

She'd always wanted a love match like her parents and sisters had. There was no doubt in her mind that she loved the arrogant oaf, but did he love her? Or was it all passion he felt for her?

She decided to be honest if that is what he wanted in a wife. "Do ye love me?"

He startled for a moment, then his face softened and he said, "Aye, lass. I love ye, and didn't realize it until just now when ye asked. Of course I want ye in my bed, but 'tis much more than that I feel for ye. Ye are smart, compassionate, funny, and I love being in yer company."

He pulled her to him with a kiss that set them both on fire. He pulled back, both of them panting. "We would be great partners, as well as lovers."

She thought for a moment, then, after taking a deep breath, looked him in the eye. "Aye, Laird Daniel Mackenzie. I will marry ye."

CHAPTER TWELVE

N O MORE THAN twenty feet from the passionate couple, Lady Chisholm tightened her lips. The bitch had managed to wangle a proposal out of the laird.

No matter, she would take care of it Alice needed a husband and her mam would get one for her. Not the one Alice wanted, but the one who would bring money, prestige, and security for both her and Lord Chisholm.

Their life would change drastically if Alice didn't marry someone like Laird Mackenzie. The invitation to come to the Castle Leod to be a possible wife to the laird had arrived at the perfect time.

She and her husband would no longer be able to keep their life together if there wasn't a new source of money.

She shook her head. Alice wanted to marry that man who had nothing, whom she claimed fathered the bairn she was carrying. *He's a hard worker* she said. So what? If her daughter thought life with a "hard worker" would be satisfying, she was living in a dream world.

Lady Chisholm did not live in a dream world. She saw their finances fading as her husband continued to drink away their funds. The gambling wasn't helping either.

They'd already raised their tenants' rents three times in the last year. There were complaints from them that they had had to sacrifice food for their bairns to pay the rent.

That wasn't her problem. They shouldn't have had so many bairns if they found it difficult to feed them. She had solved that problem by banning her husband from her bed shortly after Alice had arrived, even though he'd complained about needing an heir.

All she knew was she had to save her family, and Alice marrying Laird Daniel Mackenzie was the way to do it. Before the lass's condition became known.

There was no time to waste. The laird was obviously enamored with Lady Beth. It would take some thought and planning to keep this marriage from taking place.

Luckily, she had already secured the help of her own lady's maid, Meggie, and Joshua, the man her maid had grown attached to.

Planning, that was all it took. And Lady Chisholm was the best when it came to planning. Especially when it came to her best interests.

So, Lady Beth loved Laird Mackenzie, and he loved her. *Ach.* She thought at one time she loved her husband, but years of living with the man had changed her mind.

Now she was more interested in saving herself.

She left her hiding place in the glen and moved forward. She had a lot to do, and some of it right away before the laird approached Laird Munro and the elder advisors with his decision about a wife.

She hurried to her bedchamber and called to Meggie. "Get up, ye lazy lass. I need ye to use the handwriting ye have been practicing. And find Joshua, bring him up here to this room. We need to make haste."

Laird Daniel Mackenzie and Lady Beth Munro would not marry.

BETH PACED IN her bedchamber, her chemise whipping around her legs as she turned and moved in the opposite direction. Not that she thought she'd made the wrong decision in telling Daniel "aye," but was consumed by the fact that her entire life would change.

Mayhap she needed more time to think this through. When he was with her and holding her in his arms, she wasn't able to think straight. She'd agreed to something she'd been adamantly against for years.

Mam had stopped in a short time ago and it had been easy to see the joy on her face. Somehow even with Beth saying nothing she'd guessed that something had happened between her and Daniel.

"I doona want to talk about it," Beth said when her mam had introduced the subject.

She wasn't comfortable yet with discussing her relationship with Daniel.

After a few motherly words of wisdom that Beth didn't feel she needed, Mam had kissed her on the forehead and left her room.

Now she was tied up in knots again. Before she could convince herself that she should go to Daniel's room and discuss this further, a soft knock sounded on her door.

Knowing Mam would just walk in after one knock on the door, Beth walked to the portal and opened it.

"I ken this is no' proper, lass, but I must speak with ye a bit more." Daniel stood in the doorway, a look of confusion on his handsome face.

Before he could say anything else, she reached for the opening of his *léine* and pulled him into the room.

Neither spoke as he wrapped his arms around her and took her mouth in a searing, possessive kiss. Plastered together, he moved her farther into the room.

"Ach, love, I dinna come here to have our wedding night before the ceremony, but I had to see ye one more time before we slept."

Beth ran her hands over his mussed hair. The man must have been running his fingers through it. At a sudden thought, she pulled back. "Are ye unsure? Are ye sorry ye asked me to marry ye?"

He tugged her back again. "Nay! I never made a better choice in my life. I just wanted to be sure ye weren't having doubts before I spoke with yer dad in the morning." He ran his fingers down her cheek. "I love ye too much, Beth, to force ye into something ye really doona want. I want ye, and I've never wanted anything with this kind of ache."

THE CANDLELIGHT FROM the fire in the hearth caught the flush on her cheeks and the glint in her dark eyes—equal parts uncertainty and desire.

Daniel placed his knuckle under her chin and lifted her head. His voice low and rough, he said, "Before we continue, ye can still say nay, Beth."

She looked up at him, her throat bobbing as she swallowed. "I won't. Ye cause an ache in me, too." She stopped for a moment, then said, "Take me to bed, Daniel."

God help him.

He brushed the backs of his fingers along her jaw. Her skin was warm, impossibly soft. She trembled beneath his touch—but didn't pull away.

He cupped her face in both hands and kissed her slowly, with the control of a man barely holding himself in check. She opened for him with a sigh, her lips yielding, sweet, and curious. She tasted of honey and night-kissed air, and when her hands gripped his *léine* tugging him closer, Daniel nearly lost every shred of control.

Her breath hitched as he kissed her throat, lingering at the curve where her shoulder met her neck. Her hands slid beneath his *léine*, her palms warm and bold as they explored his chest. He groaned into her throat then caught her mouth in a kiss that was no longer gentle—hungry now, raw with need. He slid her shift up with swift, sure movements, revealing pale skin inch by inch. She stood before him like something holy, vulnerable, and unafraid.

"Sweet Mary," he muttered, staring at her with reverence. "You've undone me."

He undressed with rough efficiency, never taking his eyes off her. When he came to her again, bare skin to bare skin, she gasped—her hands splaying across his chest, fingers trembling slightly.

"Tell me what you feel," he whispered, his mouth brushing the shell of her ear.

"Everything," she breathed. "I feel everything."

He laid her on the bed, sliding over her slowly so she wouldn't feel overwhelmed. He took his time, worshipping her with lips and hands, learning the sounds she made when he kissed her breasts, when he trailed fingers along her thigh, when he whispered her name into the hollow of her neck.

Her moans were soft, but each one burned through him.

When he finally climbed between her legs, and eased inside her, he did so with care, kissing her through the brief sting, holding himself utterly still until she curled her legs around his waist and whispered, "More."

Then he moved—slow and steady at first, building a rhythm that matched her breaths, her sighs, her whispered pleas. Her nails dug into his back as her body tightened around him, and he knew he was lost.

He reached between them and circled the stiff part of her he knew would bring her the pleasure she deserved. She was wet, warm, and swollen. She began to toss her head back and forth. When he pinched the stiff flesh, she shattered beneath him with a soft cry, and after only a few thrusts, he followed, burying his face against her throat as his world broke apart in her arms.

When their breathing slowed and the room quieted again, he wrapped her tightly against him.

"I'll never let you go," he murmured into her hair. "Not now. Not ever."

Beth nestled closer, her voice thick with emotion. "I wasn't planning on leaving."

He kissed her hair and said softly, "This is not just for tonight. You ken that, doona you?"

Beth looked up, her smile soft and full of emotion. "Aye. I ken."

LADY CHISHOLM PINCHED her maid, Meggie, on the arm. "Ye have been practicing her handwriting, why now do ye say ye canno' do it?"

With tears in her eyes, the young lass looked up at her Lady. "I can do it, but I'm no' sure enough that the note would be believed."

"If ye want to keep yer position and have a roof over yer head and food in yer belly, ye better make it believable."

The lass bent over the piece of parchment Lady Chisholm had snagged from the laird's solar, along with a page from Lady Beth's journal from her room when she was out doing things a well-mannered, well-raised lass such as her Alice wouldn't do.

Lady Chisholm paced in her bed chamber while she waited for the stupid maid to finish the notes. She turned to Joshua, the man who was bedding her maid and who had agreed to help them take care of this little problem. "Things are quiet now, and the guardsmen are on the ramparts. 'Tis a good time to grab the girl and drag her to the dungeon."

With some questioning, Lady Chisholm had discovered that Castle Leod had a dungeon that hadn't been used in many years. It would be the perfect place to keep Lady Beth until the elders forced the laird to marry Alice. She didn't want to harm, or, God forbid, kill the lass, just get her out of her daughter's way.

Even when they discovered what she'd done to assure her daughter would be the next Lady Mackenzie, if they attempted to undo what had been done it would be going against the king's edict to marry either Beth or Alice by Beltane.

With the deadline, and Beth missing, marriage to Alice would be the only way to comply with the king's wishes.

Happy with the results of Meggie's notes, Lady Chisholm walked Joshua down the corridor. Just before they turned the corner, the door to the strumpet's room opened. She pushed Joshua back into a dark corner where she joined him.

Laird Makenzie walked past them, only partially dressed, which told her the situation was worse than she'd thought. It appeared the little whore thought she'd outsmart her by taking the laird to her bed.

Once she heard his bedchamber door close, she nudged Joshua and they made their way to Lady Beth's door. Lady Chisholm opened the door slowly and looked around the room.

Lady Beth was snuggled into the blankets, but with her shoulders showing, it was obvious she was without clothes. Lady Chisholm nodded to Joshua and he walked quietly to her bed. She was sound asleep. Joshua quickly wrapped his arm around her body, trapping her arms, then waved a knife in her face. Taken by surprise, the lass didn't fight him. He whispered in her ear. "Doona make a sound or yer blood will drench this bed."

Lady Beth didn't move and he dragged her off and across the room. Since the lass was naked, Lady Chisholm pulled the bedding and rolled it up the best she could. Then she placed the two notes on the bed and with a quick nod, she turned and opened the door. After quietly surveying the corridor, she waved Joshua on, him still holding the knife in front of Lady Beth's face, his other arm wrapped around her waist, her body pressed against his.

Lady Beth looked terrified, which was good because she would not make trouble if she was too scared to do anything.

The three of them made their way down the back stairs where it grew damper and wetter. Joshua had made a visit there after she had told him what she'd learned about the keep's dungeon.

Now Lady Chisholm shook with both excitement and fear. It was a dangerous thing they'd done, but Alice needed this man as her husband. Once they were married, all would be forgiven.

They continued down the stone stairs, each staircase wetter than the one before it. Mold grew on the walls and the air was so cold her shivers changed from fear and excitement to physically freezing.

Joshua finally stopped and walked about fifty feet before he stopped in front of a cell. Lady Chisholm looked around, satisfied that no one would hear the lass call for help.

She hurried past Joshua and placed some of the bedding on the floor. Once he laid Lady Beth down, Lady Chisholm covered her with the remaining bedding.

Joshua put his knife away. Lady Beth glared at her. "Ye will no' get away with this, ye ken."

Lady Chisholm laughed. "Aye. All I need is some time. Once Laird Mackenzie and my daughter are married, I will have ye released. As the wife of the laird, I expect no consequence for my Alice."

"And what about ye? Do ye think ye will have the same status as yer daughter? Do ye think the laird will no' petition the king to have the marriage annulled?"

'Twas something Lady Chisholm hadn't given thought to. "Nay. My daughter is irresistible. Laird Mackenzie will consummate the marriage straightaway."

Lady Chisholm bent over Lady Beth. "Ye will convince the laird to stay married to my daughter, or ye will suffer for it."

The lass glared at her and Lady Chisholm backed up and turned to Joshua. "Come, we must leave and get some sleep. Tomorrow will be an exciting day!"

With those words the two of them left the dungeon cell. Lady Beth began screaming after them. 'Twas no use. Joshua had tested it.

No one would hear her.

CHAPTER THIRTEEN

I T HAD BEEN two hours since Daniel had broken his fast and he still hadn't seen Beth. He'd asked after Lord Munro to set up a meeting with him, but he was out with Lord Chisholm, most likely shooting, which seemed to be their favorite pastime since they'd arrived.

Frustrated at the lack of tying things up to get the advisors—who had already sent two messages to him—off his back, he decided to go for a ride to clear his mind.

He knew the deadline of Beltane had been yesterday. But he had no intention of speaking with them until he'd first seen Lord Munro.

Beth was most likely sleeping late. He smiled, thinking the lass was probably worn out after her introduction to lovemaking.

First he stopped at the lists to make sure the training was going well. Satisfied that everything was well there, he tacked his horse and left.

Everything was going well. His feelings for Beth grew stronger every day and after last night, he couldn't wait for the wedding to be over so he could have her in his bed every night.

For an untried lass, she was very responsive which, given what he'd learned of his wife-to-be so far, was no surprise.

The air was cool, typical for early May. He rode past the bonfire from the night before, and several of the clan members cleaning up the area. No matter how much he tried to concentrate on other things, problems he needed to resolve, his mind always wandered back to his future wife.

Not too far into the future, if he had his way.

He had to smile at how everything today seemed brighter. The clan's people he met seemed more cheerful, the vendors setting up their wares smiled more, and even the smells coming from the bakery had his stomach growling.

He stopped and spent time speaking with Freda and Enoch, the owners of the bakery. They were excited to talk about the Beltane celebration the night before.

After leaving them, he began to feel guilty. He had many issues to deal with and he was wasting time riding around like some lovesick lad. It was time to return to the castle and find Beth, see if her da had returned, and get on with his life.

He was about ten minutes from Castle Leod when a man rode toward him, waving his arm to get his attention. Frowning, Daniel pulled up on Atlas's reins. "Is there is a problem, Ezra?"

"I doona ken, laird. I was asked by Lady Munro to ride to the village and find ye."

Mayhap she and Beth were planning the wedding and wanted some questions answered. "Thank ye, lad."

After leaving his horse with the stable master, he took the stairs to the keep, two at a time, to the great hall. He stopped one of the maids and asked after Lady Munro.

"Aye, laird. She is in yer solar and wishes to see ye the minute ye returned."

The fact that she waited in his solar was unusual. He opened the door to the room to see Lady Munro sitting on one of the chairs, holding papers in her hand. It was obvious she was upset and had been crying.

After closing the door, he walked toward her. Without saying anything, she held out one of the papers to him.

⟫⟫⟫✦⟪⟪⟪

LADY JEAN MUNRO had arisen that morning with a very good feeling. The king's deadline for Laird Mackenzie to choose a wife had been yesterday. Last night, she'd seen Beth and the Mackenzie strolling around the bonfire together, hands joined.

Jean had watched her other daughters with their husbands before they married and the look in their eyes was the same as she saw in the eyes of her youngest daughter and the laird.

Despite her protests about marriage and her reluctance to reconcile herself to this trip to Castle Leod, Beth was in love. And unless she was mistaken, Laird Mackenzie was in love, also.

Like most mothers, she wanted to see all her children settled with a home and family of their own. She was unhappy that her husband had chosen to go shooting with Lord Chisholm this morning. She asked him to put it off, but was reluctant to share her thoughts with him about Laird Mackenzie most likely wanting to meet with him.

Men were so dense.

With the help of her maid, Bridget, she'd risen, washed, and dressed.

"Ye seem quite happy today, my lady," Bridget said as she pulled a brush through Jean's hair, then fastened it in a chignon at the back of her neck.

"Aye, I am, Bridget. I feel today will be a wonderful day."

The young maid smiled. "Would this have anything to do with Lady Beth?"

Jean smiled. "Aye. Mayhap."

"I saw her and The Mackenzie strolling around the bonfire last night. They looked verra happy."

"They did, didn't they?" She couldn't help but share a smile with the maid.

Once she was ready to face her—hopefully happy—day, Jean left her bedchamber. She stopped outside Beth's room to see if she was ready to go down to break her fast, but decided not to trouble her. She and The Mackenzie might have been out late and the lass needed her sleep.

About two hours later, Jean was still waiting for Beth to join them. Lady Chisholm was unusually quiet, which was quite pleasant, but rare. Lady Alice, sitting next to her mam, was her usual quiet self, spending most of her time staring at her food.

"Where is the laird this morning?" Lady Chisholm asked one of the serving maids.

Jean wondered the same thing. He was generally in the great hall in the morning. But perhaps and most likely he was out on the lists, where he spent most of his time when he wasn't dealing with clan issues.

And then Bridget came rushing into the great hall, looking upset. She walked up to Jean. "My lady, may I have a word with ye?"

Jean stood and walked around the table and joined the lass who held two pieces of parchment in her hand. "What is it, Bridget?"

Completely against her usual behavior, the young maid put her arm around Jean's waist. "We must return to Lady Beth's bedchamber immediately."

BETH AWOKE COLD and confused. She placed her fingers at her throat, which felt exceedingly dry. It was very dark wherever she was. Whatever happened?

Then it all came back to her in a flash. She'd been kidnapped! Lady Chisholm had appeared in her bedchamber with some man who had dragged her naked from her bed.

She could hear water dripping and smell the dampness of something underground. She shivered at the sound of the skittering and squeaking of rodents who were probably not happy with their new guest.

Her surroundings told her she was in a dungeon. She was so scared when it all happened that she wasn't completely sure where this dungeon was.

Then she shook herself, remembering what had happened after they'd dragged her from her bed. They went down—stairs after stairs, until she thought they would be going outside.

Then Lady Chisholm had said she would remain hidden until Daniel married Lady Alice.

She knew the woman was unbalanced, but it appeared she was actually deranged.

Beth shifted around and realized Lady Chisholm had at least brought her bedding with her so she wouldn't freeze. She had wrapped herself in it during the night. Now she stood and shook it out to see what vermin slept with her.

Her shift fell to the floor. Apparently when the woman rolled up all the bedding, her shift, that Daniel had removed, got caught up in the bundle. After shaking it out, thankful to have something with which to cover her body, she slipped it over her head.

More awake now, and starting to think about her predicament, she wrapped the bedding around her and began to shout. Someone had to hear her.

All she heard was her voice coming back at her, bouncing off the walls. She swallowed a few times, trying to keep the panic away.

Lady Chisholm said she would remain here until Daniel married Lady Alice. Since yesterday had been the deadline according to the king's edict, and with Beth missing, it appeared Lady Chisholm thought Daniel would marry Lady Alice instead, switching brides like he was choosing a pair of shoes.

She had more faith in Daniel than to think he would do that. However, it did make her wonder what Lady Chisholm had planned to have Daniel do as she wished.

Beth shivered and spent time yelling again, until her throat became more sore without any water to ease the pain. She leaned against the wall and slid to a heap on the floor, tears running down her cheeks.

She brushed at something else crawling up her arm.

Daniel. Can your heart hear mine? Please, come for me. I'm scared and I doona want ye to go along with the unbalanced woman's plan.

I love ye.

⇒⟫⟪⇐

DANIEL GLANCED DOWN at the papers Lady Munro held fisted in her hand.

"What is that?"

She shook her head and held one of the papers out to him. With a shaky hand he reached out and took it. His eyes scanned the note addressed to him.

I am sorry, my laird, but I have decided to visit my sister who is not too far from here. I have to think things over. Please don't come after me.

Beth

It took him all of ten seconds to say to Lady Munro, "This is fake."

She wiped the tears from her cheeks. "How would ye ken?"

Since he no plans to tell her mother that he and her daughter had anticipated their wedding vows the night before, he merely said, "I asked Beth to marry me last evening and she was quite certain when she said yes. I have no reason to believe she's changed her mind. And especially to be so foolish as to ride off in the middle of the night."

Lady Munro jumped up. "We must go to my daughter Lady Alisa Grant's home and see if Beth is there. If she is no', then where is she?" She began wringing her hands and walking in circles.

"May I see yer note?" He reached out and Lady Munro handed him her wrinkled, damp parchment.

It was a note similar to his, just as short. He slapped the document against his hand. "I doona like this. There are several reasons I find these to be fake." Before she started to speak he added, "However, I will ride to Castle Grant and fetch Beth back if she is there."

He closed his eyes briefly and thought of the look on Beth's face when she reached her women's pleasure and afterwards when he held her in his arms. There was no doubt she was certain enough to not change her mind so quickly.

Their walks around the bonfire and the bed sport following had left a tired and satisfied Beth sound asleep when he'd climbed from her bed and returned to his bedchamber so as not to be discovered.

However, he didn't think it necessary to tell Lady Munro why he was certain Beth wasn't visiting her sister. Since he had few ideas as to where the lass was, the ride would give her mam some peace and him time to quell the panic and clear his mind.

Without raising notice, he ordered the castle and the keep searched. If that didn't turn the lass up, the men he'd dispensed were to search the woods, abandoned bothies, and every tree and blade of grass from the castle to the village.

He also requested another horse readied since he planned to ride as quickly as possible, and Atlas was most likely worn out from their morning trek. So as not to cripple the animal, it would take him two to three days each way to make the journey to Castle Grant.

He slapped his fist in his palm. He was wasting time riding to Beth's sister. But to calm Lady Munro down, it had to be done.

Lady Chisholm was sitting in the great hall, embroidery on her lap that she was ignoring as he strode through the room. However, she was giving *him* a great deal of attention.

He knew in his heart that she had something to do with Beth's disappearance and it scared him to death that while he was riding back and forth to Castle Grant, Beth was most likely in danger.

The idea came to him while he was getting travel food from Cook to bring with him. He swiftly turned from the kitchen and hurried out to the lists.

He signaled Gregory over from where he was working with a young new warrior. He jogged up to him, wiping sweat from his forehead with the palm of his hand.

"What do ye need, Daniel?"

Daniel studied him for a moment, considering his plan and deciding it was the best thing to do. He wrapped his arm around his cousin's shoulder. "I need ye to take a trip to Castle Grant."

✦

CHAPTER FOURTEEN

"YE KEN THE king ordered the laird to marry by Beltane, which ye ken was yesterday." Lady Chisholm was trying hard not to raise her voice since she didn't want others in the keep to hear her. The elders just stared at her. She couldn't leave Lady Beth in the dungeon too long.

"Lady Chisholm, we are well aware of the king's edict. However, although we've sent for the laird, he has yet to address us," Morgan said.

"He is no' here."

Abraham raised his brows. "Where is he?"

Not sure how much to tell them since she wanted them to make a quick decision, she shrugged. "I doona ken. But I believe he will be gone for a few days."

She leaned over the table and tapped the table with her finger. "I suggest ye send a missive to the king that Laird Mackenzie has decided to marry Lady Alice Chisholm and get the wedding underway before ye face the king's wrath."

"Nay, Lady Chisholm." The laird entered the solar, glaring at her.

She sucked in a breath. "I thought ye were traveling to Castle Grant?"

"And why would I be doing that?"

She didn't care for the way he studied her. Even if he knew

she'd had Beth hidden, the advisors would have to insist on the wedding to Alice to avoid whatever consequence the king would consider.

Lady Chisolm pulled her skirts close to her body and swept past him. Before she left the room, she turned to the old men. "I am merely trying to keep the Mackenzie clan from suffering at the king's hand."

DANIEL WATCHED THE woman leave the room.

Abraham pointed his finger at Daniel. "Lady Chisholm has a point, Laird. The king expected ye to be married by yesterday. Marry Lady Alice and be done with it."

"I have no intention of marrying Lady Alice Chisholm. Lady Beth Munro is my choice. I have proposed to her and she has accepted."

Morgan perked up. "So we are able to plan the wedding and send word to the king?"

Daniel tightened his lips. "Yes. But now it seems Lady Beth is missing."

"Missing?" Richard asked. "Please explain, Laird."

With no intention of speaking about last night to these men, he said, "Two notes have appeared this morning. One to Lady Munro and one to me. In those notes—which I have every reason to believe are fake—Lady Beth says she went to visit her sister at Castle Grant."

The three elder advisors all sat in silence.

Abraham tapped the table. "Then ye must marry Lady Alice and we will send word to the king."

Daniel leaned forward, his fists leaning on the table. "I will no' marry Lady Alice. Although I have no way to prove it, as I said, I believe in my heart Lady Beth's notes to her mam and myself are fake."

"If ye believe that, should ye no' be on yer way to Castle Grant and fetch yer bride?"

Daniel sighed. "I just said I believe them to be fake. However, just to make sure, I sent Gregory to Castle Grant."

Richard glared at him. "We have no idea what the king has planned for the Mackenzies if ye ignore his edict." He waved his finger at Daniel. "Ye might be making a big mistake. I say accept Lady Alice. No' everyone gets to marry who they want to."

Frustrated and getting nowhere with the men, Daniel turned and left the room, slamming the door behind him.

He left the keep and headed to the stable.

After questioning James, one of the stable lads, he learned that Gregory and a few other men had left for Castle Grant and several men had gone to search the area for Beth.

He also asked if a horse was missing. James seemed insulted that an animal could be missing and he hadn't notified the laird.

It was time for him to join the hunt. He had places that he and Beth had been to that the others would not necessarily know about.

With a heavy heart, but a strong determination, he headed out of the castle.

BETH HAD CRIED all the tears she thought could come out of her body. She even wondered if she was damaging herself since she'd had no water and couldn't afford to use up what she had with tears.

Daniel, please, listen to me. I love ye and I want to marry ye. We'll have bairns, and a wonderful life. Please don't fall for Lady Chisholms' plans, whatever they might be.

She really had no way of knowing what she'd told Daniel to go along with her plan.

Why was the woman so determined to have Daniel marry her daughter? It was obvious to anyone who had spent an hour in both their companies that Alice had no interest in becoming the laird's wife and he had no interest in her.

She laid her head down on her raised knees and tried to sleep. It might help pass the time. But for what? Would Lady Chisholm leave her in here forever to waste away, die of thirst, and be eaten by vermin?

Beth awoke with a start. Someone was outside the heavy door to her room. "Hello?" When the noise stopped, she said, "Is someone there?"

The door slowly opened and a man walked in. She was pretty sure he was the man who had dragged her on this journey to hell. Was he here to finish the job. Kill her?

She climbed to her feet. "What do you want?" Her voice was gruff, dry, painful when she spoke.

He walked a few feet toward her and she backed up. "Her ladyship doesna want ye to die."

She wiped her nose with the edge of her bedding. "How nice of her to be so considerate. If she is so concerned for my welfare, why do ye no' bring me back upstairs?"

He shrugged. "She has her reasons." He held out a mug of some type of liquid and a sack. "Here."

She took the sack and mug from him. "Is this poisoned?"

"Nay. I said she doesna want ye to die." He turned to leave.

"Wait!"

He stopped and turned back to her. He didn't say anything, just stared at her.

"Y'er the one who dragged me down here, waving a knife in my face."

He said nothing, which was no surprise.

She was about to tell him how serious the charges against him would be once she was released, but she didn't trust him not to kill her, despite what he'd said.

She turned her back on him and returned to her corner that she had cleaned out as best she could with part of the bedding.

He didn't hesitate and left the cell with no further comments.

She sighed and, preferring to make a statement by ignoring whatever food and drink had been provided, she knew in her heart Daniel was right now trying his best to find her. She didn't want him to find a dead body.

She sniffed the liquid. Ale. She looked in the sack. Bread, cheese, two apples, and cold meat.

Yes, Lady Chisholm did intend to keep her alive.

LADY CHISHOLM ENTERED Daniel's solar at his request. Without comment, he waved his hand at the chair in front of his desk.

He leaned forward, his hands resting on the desk. "Ye might think ye won by appealing to the advisors to set up a wedding with Lady Alice, but it willno' work."

Lady Chisholm sniffed. "I have no idea what ye speak of."

Daniel slammed his palms on the desk. "Aye, ye do." He took a deep breath, trying his best to get control of himself. He leaned back, his arms crossed over his chest. "Just tell me where Lady Beth is and ye, yer daughter and husband can leave Castle Leod with no consequences."

The woman gripped the arm of her chair, her face as red as the last dish of beets Daniel had eaten. "I doona ken where Lady Beth is. All I ken is what I've heard around the keep and that is she fled to her sister's home for a visit."

He stood. "Pack yer belongings and send for yer carriage. The three of ye are no longer welcomed in Castle Leod."

"Ye canno' do that!"

"I can, and I will." He stood and strode around the desk, storming from the room, slamming the door behind him.

He went to the stable and asked James to prepare Atlas for him.

The men were still out searching, but sitting around trying to get information from that despicable woman was doing no one any good.

He would join the search. She couldn't be far since she disappeared from the time he'd left her bed until the next morning.

Once his head cleared he realized having Lord and Lady Chisholm leave the castle was not the best of ideas. He was certain she was the only one who knew what had happened to Beth.

In frustration, he turned around and headed back to the castle.

"Laird, the advisors requested ye join them in the great hall when you returned." One of the grooms grabbed Atlas's reins and held him while Daniel dismounted.

As much as he hated to do it, he summoned one of the maids and asked her to have Lady Chisholm join him in his solar in about thirty minutes. That was all the time he would give the elders since he knew what they were going to say, and he didn't want to go over it again when Beth was missing and he was beginning to go from fear to absolute panic.

"Laird, have ye heard anything new?" Lady Munro walked into the great hall just as he entered. The advisors sat at the end of the dais.

He took Lady Munro's hands in his. Her hands were cold as spring water. "Nay, my lady. My men are still searching. Once I finish the meeting with these men here, I will speak one more time with Lady Chisholm, then head to the village and question everyone."

She nodded and left the room, her shoulders slumped.

Daniel took in a deep breath and walked to where the council members sat. He stood in front of them, his arms crossed over his chest. "What is it now? I have more important things to do than meet with ye every few hours. My choice of bride, who has accepted me, is missing."

Morgan held a parchment in his hand. "Ye best forget about Lady Beth, laird."

Daniel reached for the note and read it. "Nay!"

CHAPTER FIFTEEN

BETH LEANED AGAINST the slimy cold wall, tired, but unable to sleep. She'd lost count on how long she'd been in the dungeon. It seemed like forever, but was most likely two or possibly three days. It was too dark to tell if and when day had passed into night, so she couldn't be sure.

The sound of footsteps told her the man was here to bring her food and drink. It amazed her that despite what had happened to her and the horrid place in which she found herself, she was able to eat what the man brought.

The door opened and he stepped in, carrying the usual mug of ale and the sack with her food inside. Too weak to get up, she watched as he placed the candle he always carried down and handed her the mug.

Grateful for the liquid, she downed it. "I need more ale or I will die. If Lady Chisholm doesn't wish me dead, one mug of ale a day is no' going to keep me alive."

He had become more communicative with each meal he brought her. "I will bring a larger mug next time."

Beth gingerly climbed to her feet. "Do ye realize ye will be punished for this? And Lady Chisholm as well?"

The man backed up and shook his head "Nay. When Lady Alice becomes Laird Mackenzie's wife, no harm will come to her mam."

"And what about ye? The charges against ye will be as harsh as hers and ye have no connection to Lady Alice to save ye."

He handed her the sack. She wanted to keep him talking, maybe find a soft spot in the man. "And even if you doona suffer charges, what is yer benefit for doing this? Has she promised ye coin?"

He leaned on one foot, then the other, as if anxious to leave. "Lady Chisholm's maid, Meggie, is my woman. Her ladyship said she would see that we got one of the bothies to live in and both of us will work for the castle when Lady Alice marries the laird."

Beth closed her eyes and leaned against the wall. Just standing in her weak condition had black dots forming in her eyes. She sat down and looked at him. "What is yer name?"

He shifted again and narrowed his eyes. "Joshua."

"Do ye have a job here now?"

"Aye. I work in the stables and the garden."

She stared at him for a minute. "Ye say Meggie is yer woman. How would ye feel if she was treated this way? Kidnapped, locked up in a dungeon?"

He thought for a minute. "I am sorry to have done this to ye, but Meggie is determined that we marry and have our own home."

Beth shook her head. "And for the rest of yer life, ye will do what Meggie wants, even though it could cause ye harm in the end?"

Just as she imagined her comment had him thinking, he said, "I needs go now. I will bring more ale later." With those curt words, Joshua left, locking the door behind him.

Beth peered sadly at the empty mug and pulled out bread, cold meat, and cheese from the sack. No apples today. She sighed and ate slowly, her dry mouth making it hard to swallow.

She shuddered and shook her foot when what felt like a critter bit her toe. Placing the sack in her lap, she lowered her head and cried. The only thing keeping her alive now was the knowledge that Daniel would be frantic looking for her.

Hopefully, he would find her before she died.

Please Daniel. I doona ken how much longer I can survive this.

"WHO GOES THERE?" One of the guardsmen on the ramparts shouted to Gregory and the three men who came with him as they arrived at Castle Grant.

"Gregory Mackenzie, cousin to Clan Chief Daniel Mackenzie to see Lady Grant."

Silence followed for a few minutes, then the same man called out, "What is yer business with my lady?"

"I have a message from her mother, Lady Munro."

That must have thrown the man into confusion. Silence followed.

After waiting a several minutes, the castle drawbridge descended and a young woman came hurrying down the steps of the keep and into the outer bailey.

Gregory and his men rode over the drawbridge, the horses' hooves clattering. There was no mistaking the woman holding her skirts as she ran towards them was Lady Alice's sister, Lady Grant. Both were pretty, blonde, and curved in all the right places.

She ran up to them as they dismounted. "My guardsman said ye have a message from my mam?"

"Aye. But first I must ask ye if yer sister, Lady Beth Munro is here?"

The lass turned pale and shook her head. "Nay. Is she supposed to be?"

A man strode up to them. "What is this business with my wife?" He placed his protective arm around Lady Grant's waist and moved her slightly back.

"I represent Clan Chief Laird Daniel Makenzie—"

"That is where my sister and parents are right now." She turned to her husband and frowned before turning back to

Gregory. "Are they no' there?" she asked.

He could hear the slight panic in the lass's voice. Her husband hugged her closer and said to Gregory. "Ye and yer men are welcomed into our keep." Before they took one step however, he said, "Please leave yer swords here in the outer bailey. 'Tis a practice with everyone who comes to Castle Grant unexpectedly."

Gregory nodded and he and his men all withdrew their swords and other weapons and handed them to two guardsmen who stood behind them.

They followed Laird and Lady Grant to settle at a large table in the great hall. Lady Grant called for a maid to bring food and drink.

"I am hardly able to control myself. The last I heard from my sister, she and my parents were headed to Castle Leod where there was a potential betrothal. Why do ye think she is here?"

Gregory went through the story of Lady Beth's disappearance, the notes to Daniel and Lady Munro and the laird's insistence Lady Beth had already accepted his proposal and would not have scurried off to her sister's home.

"So what ye are telling me is my sister is missing," Lady Grant said, raising her chin, reminding him of Lady Beth.

Gregory hesitated but there was no reason to falter. "Since Lady Beth is no' here, then I'm afraid, aye, she is missing."

The lass sucked in a deep breath and turned to her husband, tears beginning to run down her face. He reached out and gathered her into his arms.

Laird Grant looked at Gregory as if he was the one who had something to do with the disappearance of Beth. Hopefully the laird was not of the "kill the messenger" persuasion.

Mugs of ale and a platter of dried meat, cheese, bread and butter was placed in front of them by two serving maids.

The interruption gave Lady Grant a moment to compose herself, and she said, "How is my mam?"

Gregory shrugged. "Concerned. She also is of the mind that

the notes were fake, but she agreed with Laird Mackenzie that someone should travel to Castle Grant and make sure."

"What are they doing in the meantime?" Lady Grant wiped her nose on a linen cloth and shook her head when her husband pointed at the food.

Gregory and his men filled their metal plates with the offerings. "Laird Mackenzie was going to take the trip here, but since he was so convinced that Lady Beth would no' be here, he asked me to take the journey so he and his men could do a thorough search at our own keep."

Lady Grant looked over at her husband, determination in her face. "I am going to Castle Leod."

He did not hesitate. "Nay."

"Aye."

The laird sighed. "Alisa, 'tis a two or three day journey. By the time ye get there, 'twill most likely be over and yer sister safe."

The lass glared at her husband. "I am going. My sister is missing and my mam must be beside herself. And if all is well when we get there, which I pray it will be, we can attend her wedding."

The laird's tightened lips softened and he reached out his hand to cover his wife's. "Aye. We will both go. The little ones will be fine under their nurses' care."

Lady Grant slumped in relief.

As much as Gregory didn't wish to get right back on a horse, he knew Laird and Lady Grant would want to leave as soon as possible. "May we borrow a few of yer horses? Ours are all worn out."

DANIEL RODE TO the village on Atlas as though the demons of hell were after him. He had to find Beth, and soon. Every time he thought about the missive Abraham had handed him, he grew angrier.

The king was at Invergarry Castle, home of the MacIntosh clan, where one of his sisters lived. His note said as long as he was this far north, he wanted to visit Castle Leod and congratulate the new bride and groom.

It was a three or four day trip, depending on how much equipment and supplies they carried with them and how many men rode.

Daniel had no doubt that the king was checking to make sure the wedding had taken place. The elders were pushing hard for him to marry Lady Alice. They intended to present the Laird and Lady of Mackenzie to King George II when he arrived.

If Beth was not found before the king arrived, there would be no Lady Mackenzie to present to the king. The man had given him a choice of two lasses, and he'd done what was commanded—he'd chosen one. 'Tis true he didn't make the deadline of marriage by Beltane, but once Beth was found he would be sure to have an immediate ceremony.

His fear of the king's wrath was nothing compared to his fear for Beth. Where the devil could she be?

There was no doubt in his mind now that he loved the lass. He'd been attracted to her from the time when her mam had insisted she remove the hideous costume and she'd returned as one of the most beautiful women he'd ever seen.

Her sense of humor, determination, helpfulness, and kindness pushed him further into love. As well as her sense of adventure and intense intelligence. He would have her for his wife and whoever kidnapped her—and he had his suspicions—would be punished.

He rode to the village and began questioning everyone he saw. No one had seen Beth or anything untoward. His men had been here before while Daniel had scoured every inch of land within miles of Castle Leod. Every standing structure had been searched.

After getting nowhere with his questions, and feeling frustrated, he went to the tavern for an ale.

One of the serving lasses, the daughter of the tavern owner, approached his table with a mug of ale. "Where is that sweet lass we saw ye with at the Beltane celebration?"

Daniel perked up. "Have ye seen her?"

The lass shook her head. "Nay. No' since Beltane. Is she no' here with ye today?"

He shook his head and drank half the mug of ale. "Nay. Have ye seen her in the last couple of days? Since Beltane?"

She frowned at him. "Nay. Is the lass missing?"

"Aye. If ye hear anything at all, please send someone to the castle. The word is that she may have decided to visit her sister at Castle Grant."

She nodded as one of the customers summoned her. "If I hear anything I'll let ye ken."

He finished his ale, and left, his frustration growing to un-measurable heights.

God's bones, he wished the king would stay out of his affairs. Out of *all* Scotland's affairs. 'Twas bad enough to make the edict, then send him two lasses with the command to "pick one" like he was buying a horse, set a pointless date, and *then* decide to travel to Castle Leod to make sure the deed was done.

'Twas no wonder there was talk of another uprising against the English. Highlanders wanted to govern themselves, not be told what to do by a British king.

None of that mattered now, however, since his greatest concern now was the safety of Lady Beth Munro. His intended wife. The more time she was missing, the more frightened he became.

She could not have disappeared into thin air. Again, on his way back to the stables, he stopped at each vendor and shop with a friendly reminder to send word to the castle if they learned anything.

He waved at Freda as he left the bakery. She turned as Enoch joined her in the front of the store. "Was that the laird again?"

"Aye." She wiped her hands on her apron. "I have no idea what is going up at the castle, but I doona remember a time when

Laird Mackenzie looked so frantic."

Enoch picked up the leftover loaves of bread, which they would use the next morning to make the squares of bread pudding that were so popular with their customers.

"Mayhap we should have told the laird about the man from the castle who comes here for a loaf of bread every day, then buys cheese from Farmer Malcolm's wife, heads to the village tavern and leaves there with a heavier sack. Then he heads back to the castle. It doesna seem enough to feed the keep."

Freda shrugged. "Mayhap he doesna get enough to eat at the castle. I doona see what that would have to do with the sweet lass disappearing. However, the next time he comes to the village, I will mention it to him."

She and Enoch began to clean up the work area as well as the store front.

Freda watched Laird Mackenzie at the stables as he settled on his horse and left the village, heading to the castle.

His sad demeanor saddened her as well.

CHAPTER SIXTEEN

"**B**UT LAIRD, THE king is arriving. We have no choice. He expects to meet the new Lady Mackenzie."

Daniel looked Morgan in the eye. "I doona understand why ye doona understand *me*. I will no' marry Lady Alice. I will find Lady Beth and marry her. I doona care if the king comes to the castle, or if God himself makes an appearance."

"Laird, ye are becoming unhinged. The clan needs the support of the king," Abraham said.

Weary and tired, Daniel banged his fist on the table in front of the three old men. "Doona push me. That is all I have to say about this."

Daniel turned and stormed from the room, slamming the door so hard that it rattled the walls. 'Twas time to dismiss them. He didn't need advisors.

LADY CHISHOLM STOOD in a shadow against the wall after watching the laird leave the meeting with his advisors. He'd been so angry he didn't see her, which was perfect because she wanted to speak with the elders without the laird knowing.

Hearing voices from within, she stopped before knocking on

the door, listening to what the men said.

"'Tis time to have the chatelaine prepare for the wedding," one of the men said.

Another one spoke. "Between Laird Mackenzie and who?"

"I doona ken. But there will be a wedding tomorrow no matter who stands before Father Matthew."

The three elders remained silent after that, so Lady Chisholm knocked softly on the door. After they allowed her entrance, she walked into the room and took a seat in front of the table where the men sat.

"Lady Alice is quite anxious to get the wedding underway since Lady Beth has apparently left the castle. I ken the king is on his way and I doona want The Mackenzie to have problems with the monarch."

The one she knew as Abraham leaned back in his chair. "And how is it ye ken that Lady Beth willno' return before the king arrives?"

She shrugged, attempting to appear indifferent. "No more than anyone else in the castle kens with men running all over the place looking for her. And it has been days."

After a few moments of silence, Morgan said, "We have decided to go ahead and set a wedding up for tomorrow. We expect our king to arrive in a day or two. I suggest ye get yer daughter ready to marry the laird. We canno' continue to wait for Lady Beth to appear."

Lady Chisholm hopped up, smiling brightly. "I shall speak with my daughter immediately. I will also offer yer chatelaine, Louise, my assistance with planning the wedding festivities."

Abraham nodded and waved her off.

Finally, things were going her way. She would get Alice's gown that they'd brought with them freshened up and pressed.

Back when they had received word from the king that Alice would be one of two choices for Lady Mackenzie, she'd had no intention of the laird choosing anyone else besides her daughter. And quickly.

She'd seen it as an answer to her prayers. Alice would become the laird's wife and there would be plenty of money to support her and Lord Chisholm.

And the little romance Alice was having with that common man would come to an end.

She hurried up to the bedchamber to which Alice had been assigned. "Get up ye lazy lass. I have great news for ye!"

Alice rolled over in the bed. "I doona feel so well."

Lady Chisholm strode over to her daughter and bent over. "That is yer own fault for getting yerself in this mess." She stood and placed her hands at her waist. "Ye will marry the laird tomorrow."

Alice shot up from the bed. "What! He doesna want to marry me. He wants to marry Lady Beth."

"Ye ken she has disappeared. She's run off because she doesna want to marry him."

Alice threw the bedcovers off and sat up. "I doona want to marry him either." She pulled on a dressing gown, rubbing her hands up and down her arms against the chill in the room.

"And we all ken Lady Beth is missing," she continued. "If she did run off on her own, Laird Mackenzie will find her and convince her to marry him. I just need time."

"There is no time, young lady. The king arrives in a day or two and expects to see the laird married to one of ye."

Alice crossed her arms over her chest and sat on the bed. "It willna be me."

Lady Chisholm reached out and pulled her daughter forward by her hair. "Aye, it will be ye. I'm trying to get ye out of the mess ye got yerself into. Now get dressed and meet me in the great hall. We have a wedding to plan."

GREGORY, ALONG WITH Laird and Lady Grant, rode into the outer bailey shortly after sunrise. It had been a gruesome trip back from Castle Grant. They had selected three of the sturdier horses from the Grant stable for the trip.

At Lady Grant's insistence they only slept for a few hours and took short breaks through the days mostly to give their horses a rest.

"Is Lady Beth here?" she asked as Laird Grant helped her from her horse.

The stable lad shook his head. "Nay."

The poor lass looked as though she would collapse. "Where can I find Lady Munro?"

Gregory waved at a maid. "See that Lady Grant is taken to her mam's bedchamber. Also have food and drink brought in for our guests."

Rubbing his hand over his face, he left the couple in the great hall, Laird Grant appealing to his wife to have something to eat before she sought out her mam.

Gregory went in search of Daniel.

He found Daniel in his solar where the laird was attempting to drink himself into a coma.

Gregory grabbed the mug of whisky from in front of his cousin, took a jug of cold water from the table, and poured it over his head. "Ye need yer senses if ye're going to find the lass."

Daniel shook his head, water from his hair flying in every direction. "Nay. Were I no' a gentleman, I would put Lady Chisholm on the rack and get answers from her."

Gregory settled in the chair across from him. "So sure ye are that she has something to do with Lady Beth's disappearance?"

Daniel rubbed his bloodshot eyes. "Aye. 'Tis impossible that Beth changed her mind, and since ye are here in front of me without her, I assume she was no' at her sister's keep as the note stated."

Gregory nodded. "Laird and Lady Grant traveled back with me. Beth's sister is verra concerned and wanted to offer comfort to her mam."

Daniel looked out the window at the sunny day. Not very sunny for him. "And Lady Chisholm was much too quick to confer with the elders about Lady Alice being the chosen bride. Like she kenned that Lady Beth was well-hidden or, I pray not, dead."

Gregory winced at Daniel's statement. "From what I heard in the bailey just now, the king will probably arrive some time tomorrow. Lady Chisholm is planning a wedding. What do ye plan to do?"

"I doona care about the king. Beth has been missing for days now."

Daniel laid his head on his desk and within minutes he was snoring. Gregory assumed the man hadn't slept more than a few hours since Lady Beth had disappeared.

He left the room and quietly closed the door.

LATER THAT DAY, Daniel awoke and, feeling gritty and still tired, walked to the loch where he removed his clothes and dove into the cold water. It startled him awake better than anything else would have done.

He swam until his muscles ached. He eventually climbed from the water and shook himself off like a wet dog, then dried his body with his clothes, putting the damp articles back on.

He continued his search for Beth, frantically turning over every rock, and climbing over every decrepit bothy and abandoned wagon on his land. He called her name until his throat ached.

The sun was making its descent in the western sky as he made his way back to the keep. Gregory stood at the end of the drawbridge, his hands on his hips. "Cousin, I am becoming concerned for yer mind."

From what he could see when he entered the keep, Lady

Chisholm was driving everyone crazy planning a wedding that no one wanted. He'd heard the staff felt a liking for quiet Lady Alice, but they all loathed Lady Chisholm who had made it clear she would take up residency once her daughter was married to the laird.

Lady Chisholm stood in front of him, blocking his way. "'Tis about time ye returned to the keep, Laird. Ye are getting married tomorrow, hopefully before the king arrives. There are things ye need to do and decisions to be made."

Holding himself from pushing the woman out of the way, he said, "There will be no wedding tomorrow unless Lady Beth is standing beside me. I doona ken how many times and how many people I need to say this to."

Her jaw tightened. "The king arrives tomorrow."

"Then let *him* marry Lady Alice." He moved away from her, before he put his hands on the woman, something he never did in his life and ever expected to.

He was near the steps to the upper floor when a young maid came racing down the stairs. "Lady Chisholm!"

"What!" Her snarl had the maid backing up.

"Lady Alice is gone." The young girl stood wringing her hands.

Daniel burst out laughing as he turned toward the stairs, wishing with all his might that this nightmare would end.

ALISA SAT ON the floor, her head on her mam's lap. "I doona understand. Where can Beth be if the laird has searched everywhere in the keep and the Mackenzie lands?"

Lady Munro ran her hand down her face. "My mother's instinct says she is somewhere in this castle."

"This is truly frightening," Alisa said.

Her mam sighed. "Aye, and there are those of us who believe

Lady Chisholm has something to do with it."

Alisa looked up at her mam. "Has she been questioned?"

"Extensively, but she holds that he kens no'hing about Beth's disappearance."

Alisa thought for a minute. "What about the notes that were left? Could you tell if it was Beth's handwriting?"

Tears appeared in her mam's eyes and she blotted the corners with a linen she carried. "I showed them to yer da and we both agreed it was an imitation of her handwriting." She smiled softly. "The laird took one look at the note that was left for him and he announced it was a fake. Since I doubt he had time to study her handwriting the short time we've been there, it makes me wonder if there is something between them I don't ken about."

"Then this was planned for a while if someone had the time to practice her handwriting."

Her mam smoothed her daughter's hair from her forehead. "I am verra afraid daughter. I fear I haven't prayed hard enough."

The yelling and screaming coming from the great hall was loud enough to reach Alisa and her mam. "That sounds like Lady Chisholm," Alisa said.

"Now what?" her mam muttered. "The woman is such a difficult person."

As they descended the stairs, Lady Chisholm's hands were fisted in Laird Mackenzie's *léine*. "Ye must find my daughter. The king will arrive at any time."

He disengaged her hands from him. "Ye must be out of yer mind. Lady Beth has been missing for days and ye want me to spend time looking for yer daughter?" He leaned in close to the woman's face. "Especially since I believe ye ken where Lady Beth is."

Lady Chisholm covered her face with her hands and wailed. "Ye must find her. She's to marry tomorrow."

Shaking his head in disgust, Daniel walked out of the keep.

Lady Chisholm turned to the group who had gathered. "My daughter is missing. Someone must find her."

No one spoke or moved.

A man's voice called from the outer bailey. "The king has arrived!"

CHAPTER SEVENTEEN

"LADY ALICE IS missing now, too?" Morgan glared at Gregory as if he were the one responsible for another lass gone.

"Aye. She is nowhere in the castle and her mam says a satchel with her clothes is gone from her bedchamber."

"And the king is here?" Abraham asked, drumming his fingers on the table in front of him.

Gregory nodded. "He just arrived with his people. Lady Chisholm has the wedding planned for tomorrow."

"With who? Both lasses the king sent are gone." Abraham turned to Richard. "We are cursed."

"Where is the laird while all this is going on?" Morgan asked.

"The same place he's been for the last few days. Questioning everyone in the village, searching everywhere, angrier than a bear with an arrow in its arse."

"Has he at least greeted the king?" Richard asked.

Gregory nodded. "Briefly. He made sure accommodations were ready for the king and his party, then after checking with the cook that food and drink was available, he left again."

Richard ran his hand down his face. "We have a wedding planned for tomorrow, a ferocious almost unhinged groom roaming the land, a missing bride, and a king expecting to meet the new Lady Mackenzie since he would assume his edict had been followed."

Abraham looked over at Richard. "*Two* missing brides."

JOSHUA GREW MORE nervous as the days went by with Lady Beth still in the dungeon. He'd gone every day, sometimes twice with ale and food, but she looked awful.

Most times he had to stay there and make sure she ate what he brought her. She had lost her initial spirit from when they first put her there. His sympathy for the lass, and for the laird who was frantically looking for her, was increasing every day.

When he agreed to do this for the benefit of marrying Meggie and having a place of his own and a living for the rest of his life, it didn't seem to be a problem.

He never would have guessed that the lass would be stuck in the dungeon so long. He knew Lady Chisholm wanted the laird to marry her daughter, but Joshua hadn't known that the man was so against it.

It was Lady Chisholm who had come up with the plan to kidnap her and had Meggie ask him to help. She'd had him search the castle and find a place where Lady Beth could be held that no one would find.

By asking questions, he learned that there was a dungeon in the castle that hadn't been used for years. After investigating the place himself, he presented the information to Lady Chisholm.

She once again agreed that in payment for him helping, she would see that Lady Alice would provide a bothy for him and Meggie once they were married, as well as permanent jobs for them both.

Once they arrived at Lady Beth's bedchamber the night they took her, he refused to hold a knife to her throat, but Lady Chisholm had insisted it was the only way to keep the lass quiet as they moved her through the keep. To appease both his conscience and Lady Chisholm's demands, he merely waved the knife at Lady Beth's face.

He needed to speak with Meggie since she saw Lady Chisholm every day and he needed to find out when this would all end. But every time he tried to speak with Meggie, she was always too busy and said she would talk to him later.

Later never happened and now he was growing both anxious and angry. He needed to know how much longer they would keep Lady Beth in the dungeon. He saw how she was suffering, and they did not. After what he'd seen and heard from Lady Chisholm, she wouldn't care, anyway.

Things had become crazier with the king arriving and Lady Alice also disappearing. He wished he'd never become involved with Lady Chisholm. He should have found a way to get a house by himself for him and Meggie.

He had skills and could have found a way to support them, too.

Joshua had been attracted to Meggie from the time she'd arrive with Laird and Lady Chisholm. She was a black-haired beauty who had caught the attention of a number of the Mackenzie warriors.

When she asked him to help with kidnapping Lady Beth, he knew it was his way to get her for himself.

The best way he could speak with Meggie would be to catch her in the small maid's room once everyone in the keep was asleep.

Joshua made his way quietly to her room when things finally appeared to be settled down with the king retiring to his chambers and Lady Chisholm receiving a potion from Emma, the healer, to quiet her nerves.

He knocked softly on Meggie's door and then opened it, assuming she was asleep.

She was not asleep.

Meggie was enjoying very enthusiastic bed sport with Damon, one of the guardsmen.

CHAPTER EIGHTEEN

THE NEXT MORNING, the king looked around the great hall. "Why have I seen so little of The Mackenzie?"

Laird Grant, Laird Munro, Laird Chisholm, and Gregory all sat at the dais with the king and several of his men, attempting to make everything appear normal. The room was filled with clan people, the air exceptionally quiet and tense.

"He is quite busy with the wedding." Laird Chisholm hiccupped.

The king looked down the dais. "And where are all the women?"

"The wedding," Laird Grant mumbled.

The king nodded at the young serving maid who was pouring ale into the mugs on the table. "I thought I ordered the wedding to take place on Beltane?"

Gregory cleared his throat. "Aye, your majesty, but circumstances made it difficult to do it on that exact day."

The king frowned. "What circumstances? It was my order. I am your king."

Gregory hesitated. "Border problems, your majesty." He gulped some of his ale.

The king sat back, his arms resting on his considerable middle. "I should have been informed of any border issues."

Hopefully the king would become more interested in his food

and stop throwing out questions Gregory didn't want to answer.

"Aye. I believe Laird Mackenzie intended to inform ye when ye arrived since that would be faster than sending a messenger to Kensington Palace with ye expected here shortly."

The king nodded. "And which of the lovely ladies has the laird chosen for his wife?"

Silence reigned both at the dais and the entire great hall, all eyes on Gregory. He fumbled for a minute, then said, "I believe the laird wishes to make it a surprise for ye."

Whether the king believed that or not, he didn't say, but merely picked up his eating knife and continued his meal.

St. Agnes's armpit. How were they going to get out of this? Eventually the king would have to be told that both lasses were missing. It was good luck that the healer, Emma, had given Lady Chisholm a potion the night before, and then again this morning Meggie gave her another one. Otherwise, she would be here right now wailing and beating her breast, throwing herself at the king's feet.

Even though Daniel had refused to look for Lady Alice until Lady Beth was found, he did send out a number of men to search for the lass. Since she'd left with a satchel full of her belongings, and no horse was missing from the stables, it appeared she had not been forced to go and was most likely meeting someone.

Gregory would have loved to make normal conversation with the king, but he could think of nothing to say that wouldn't make things uncomfortable. Thankfully, his men kept him occupied.

DANIEL SAT IN his solar. Another day of searching with no result. And now with Lady Alice also missing, the nightmare was becoming even worse.

It had been about five days since Beth had been found missing. His faith in finding her safe and sound was slowly webbing from panic into anger.

He ran his hand down his face and looked out the window. He turned toward the door at the sound of a soft knock. "Enter."

A young man cautiously walked into the room, his face pale as new milk. He cleared his throat. "Good morn, my laird."

Daniel nodded and waved to the chair in front of his desk. "Ye look familiar, but I am afraid I doona remember yer name."

"'Tis Joshua, my laird. I work in the stables and the gardens."

It was very obvious the young man was nervous. "Ye seem a tad uncomfortable. If ye have something to say, just do it. I have to be out looking for Lady Beth."

Joshua shook his head. "Nay."

Daniel's stomach dropped to his feet. "What do ye mean?"

The young man took a deep breath. "Ye doona have to keep searching for her."

Daniel stood, towering over him. "Ye better say whatever it is ye came to say."

Joshua closed his eyes and answered in a whisper. "I ken where Lady Beth is."

Before he could stop himself, Daniel jumped over the desk and wrapped his arms around Joshua's neck. "Ye better speak and speak fast."

"She's in the dungeon. Lady Chisholm had me bring her there." His high-pitched voice was full of fear.

Daniel shook his head, hoping to clear it. "The dungeon under the castle that hasn't been used in about fifty years?"

"Aye."

Daniel let go of him, grabbed his *léine* in his fist, and dragged him to the solar door. "Show me." He shoved him out of the room.

Joshua hurried down the stairs, Daniel right behind him. His mind was in a whirl. All this time Lady Beth was here in the castle? In the dungeon? After five days she could have starved to death.

After three, she could have died from lack of water.

The two of them raced through the great hall, ignoring everyone at the dais and shouts from Gregory. Stopping abruptly, he looked over at his cousin. "Get Emma. Have her go to the bedchamber Lady Beth was assigned." When the man just stared at him, he yelled, "Now!"

His heart pounded as they descended the slimy, cold, smelly stairs. Just as he believed the lad was leading him to his own death, Joshua turned and headed down a corridor, both of them slipping and sliding on the moss-covered ground as they moved as fast as they could. Joshua stopped at one of the cells, removed the bar and flung the door open.

Daniel immediately spotted someone curled up in the corner. Having been in the dark staircase, his eyes had adjusted and he recognized Beth wrapped in a filthy blanket. He squatted next to her and with a howl of agony, scooped her into his arms. "Get me out of here," he growled at Joshua.

They went back the way they came. Daniel didn't have time to stop and see what shape Beth was in, or if she was even still alive. He just had to get her out this hellhole.

When they arrived at the great hall, he shouted to Gregory, "Put Lady Chisholm under house arrest and get Lady Munro and Lady Grant and have them go to Beth's bedchamber."

Just as he hit the bottom of the stairs, Emma came racing into the great hall, her basket of medicants over her arm. "I'm here, Laird, just tell me what to do."

He nodded and she asked no questions, just followed Daniel up the stairs. He burst into Beth's bedchamber, thinking of the night he'd made love to her in this very room. He prayed with everything he had that they had saved her in time.

"God's bones!" Emma said as Daniel placed Beth on the bed. He placed his fingers on her neck and took the first solid breath since Joshua had appeared in his solar. Her pulse was weak, but steady.

As Emma approached the bed, Daniel turned to Joshua. "Go

to the great hall and stay there until I come for ye."

Still pale as snow, the lad nodded and left the room.

Lady Grant and Lady Munro raced into the room. "Did ye find Beth?"

"Aye. She was in the dungeon."

Lady Munro covered her mouth, tears forming in her eyes. "Is she…dead?" She grabbed Lady Grant's hand.

"Nay. Emma is about to examine her."

Emma looked briefly at Beth and turned her attention to him. "Laird, ye are going to have to leave the room, I need to undress Lady Beth."

He shook his head clenching her hand. "Nay. I am not leaving until she opens her eyes and speaks to me."

Emma's eyes widened. "'Ye canno' stay, Laird. I need to get down to her skin to see about insect and rodent bites."

He gritted his teeth. "I am the laird and I am no' leaving."

Lady Grant and Lady Munro looked at each other. He turned to Beth's mam. "As soon as Beth awakens she will become my wife. Therefore, I am no' leaving her."

Emma touched him on his arm. "I ken ye are overwrought Laird, but 'tis no' proper for ye to stay."

"Fine. Send for Father Matthew and he can marry us right now."

"The lass is unconscious!"

He spread his feet in a show of defiance. The three women looked at each other. Lady Munro stepped up to Emma. "Doona make a fuss, lass. Let him stay. We can no longer delay seeing to my daughter."

Her chemise was filthy and it was obvious she had emptied her stomach on herself. Probably more than once.

Daniel closed his eyes at the condition of the woman he loved. Lady Chisholm would hang for murder if Beth died. Then he said a quick prayer that Beth would return to him.

Once Emma had removed all her clothes, she laid a piece of linen over Beth's breasts and private parts. She turned to Lady

Grant. "My lady, I hate to make a servant out of ye, but I need a pan of warm water, some strong soap and clean cloths."

As Lady Grant left the room, Emma turned to Lady Munro. "I will need a clean nightgown to put on Lady Beth."

Both women left the room and Emma looked over to Daniel. "I doona think Lady Beth is in mortal danger, but some of these bites can cause infections. Plus, depending on whether she got food and liquids while held captive, it may take her time to recover."

Daniel gritted his teeth. "I doona care how long it takes or what effort or expense is involved. Just save my…" The words became trapped in his throat, as if he were choking. He turned, and headed to look out of the window so Emma couldn't see his tears.

LADY CHISHOLM SNARLED at Meggie. "I thought ye said yer lover was to be trusted!"

Her maid cowered in Lady Chisholm's bedchamber as the woman came at her with a fire iron in her hand.

Gregory Mackenzie had just left her bedchamber after telling her she was under house arrest for abducting Lady Beth Munro.

"I am Lady Chisholm, I canno' be held in house arrest," she'd blustered to Gregory. "I fear the laird has lost his mind."

The man turned from her in disgust and left the room. Meggie walked the outer area of the space, trying her best to avoid the crazed woman.

Lady Chisholm was angry that no one seemed to be concerned that *her* daughter was missing. If that lass had left the castle to meet up with that lover of hers, she would see her left without any help or support from her parents when it all fell apart.

Support? Since the laird had recovered Lady Beth there would be no wedding between him and her daughter. They would now live in penury. Or worse at the behest of her husband's relatives, who despised her.

Someone would pay for this. Either her daughter, her lover, her maid, or the *idjit* lad that Meggie had told her was a man who she had under her control.

CHAPTER NINETEEN

After getting Beth bathed and into a clean, fresh night-gown, and changing the bedding to avoid infestation, Lady Munro and Lady Grant's husbands persuaded them to return to the great hall for supper.

When the men suggested Daniel join them as well, he refused. "Have someone send up food. I am no' leaving until Beth wakes up."

Emma had said there were no serious injuries, but the lass had suffered insect and rodent bites. She also needed food and drink. He'd attempted to feed her broth and ale. Sometimes she would sip it, but never seemed to fully awaken.

Instead of meeting with Joshua downstairs in the great hall, he sent for the lad to present himself to Lady Beth's bedchamber.

Gregory stopped on his way to supper and spoke to him about King George. Apparently the king was insulted because he'd sent an order for Daniel to meet with him to explain what was going on, but Daniel refused and sent word to the king he was more than welcome to come to Beth's bedchamber to meet with him.

The lad crept into the room looking quite unsettled. "Laird, ye wished to speak with me?"

"Aye, lad. I would like the entire story of how Lady Beth ended up in the dungeon, and why ye chose to tell me about it after she'd been there for five days."

The lad looked as if he was about to bring up his last meal onto his shoes "Lady Chisholm's maid, Meggie and I had formed an attachment."

When it seemed the lad would stop, Daniel shrugged and waved at Joshua to continue.

"She brought me to see Lady Chisholm one day and she asked me to take Lady Beth to a hiding place and once Lady Alice married the laird," he gulped, "um, *you*—she would see that Meggie and I would get a small house and permanent jobs."

Daniel ran his hand down his face. "So ye sold out yer laird for a bothy? And a job? Even though ye already had a job in the stables?"

The lad grew even more pale.

"Did ye then leave Lady Beth there to starve? Did ye no' worry about her in that cold dark place?" He could feel his temper rising as he spoke with the lad.

"Nay!" He cried. "I went every day and brought her food and drink, and the last two days I went in the morning and then in the evening. At that point I had to sit there and make sure she ate."

"What made ye decide to tell me?" Daniel was having a hard time understanding this lad. Was he evil? Greedy? Caring?

"I went to see Meggie to tell her that Lady Beth was growing weaker every day and asked when would ye marry Lady Alice so we could bring Lady Beth up."

"I never had any intention of marrying Lady Alice."

He nodded. "I dinna ken it at the time. Lady Chisholm made it sound like ye wanted her daughter, and Lady Beth was only a distraction, and once she was gone for a day or so, yer wedding to Lady Alice would take place."

Daniel thought for a moment about the treachery of Lady Chisholm. "Did Meggie agree with ye then to release Lady Beth?"

Joshua remained silent for a moment. "I never got to speak with her about that."

Daniel raised a questioning brow.

"I found her in her bed with another mon."

BETH OPENED HER eyes at the sound of Daniel's voice. "Daniel?" She didn't recognize herself, so raspy was the noise coming from her throat.

His large body moved across the room to the bed in seconds. "Beth." He took her hand in his and closed his eyes. "Ye'r awake."

"Am I still in in the dungeon? Is that Joshua's voice I hear?" Fatigued from just that bit of conversation, she closed her eyes again.

"Nay, my love, ye are no longer in the dungeon, I carried ye to yer bedchamber. Joshua led me to where ye were."

She closed her eyes and kissed his knuckles where he gripped her hand so tightly. "I ken ye would come for me."

He smiled softly at her. "I will ne'er leave ye and always come for ye. I love ye, Lady Beth Munro."

A tear slid down her cheek. "I love ye, too." She smiled at how easily those words came from her thick throat. "Can ye help me sit up? I would like to have a drink."

Daniel turned to Joshua. "Ye can leave me now. Go to the kitchen and have a maid bring up food and ale for Lady Beth. However, do no' return to yer duties in the stables. Remain in the great hall."

Joshua paled again, and nodded. "Aye, Laird."

Daniel placed his hand under her back, the warmth from his hand soothing her body which still felt chilled from her time in the dungeon.

Once she was settled against several fluffy pillows, Daniel sat alongside her and smiled in that special way, and cupping her face in his hands, appeared about to give her a kiss when the door burst open and her mam and sister raced into the room.

"'Tis true?" Beth's mam asked. "Beth is awake?"

Beth smiled at the disappointment on Daniel's face. He moved back, allowing her mam and Alisa to sit on the edge of her bed.

He smoothed the hair back on her forehead. "I will return in a little bit while ye visit with yer sister and mam. I need to speak with the king and settle his ruffled feathers."

Beth reached out and grabbed his hand, her eyes full of tears, suddenly very frightened. "Please doona leave."

"I willna be long, and then I will stay with ye all night." He looked at Lady Munro. "Please doona leave Beth by herself. I won't be long. Try to get her to eat."

Mam wiped the tears from her eyes and took Beth's hand in hers. "Ye will be fine until the laird returns."

She nodded, feeling verra strange about him leaving her. Hopefully as time passed, she would get over this distress of being without him.

The door to the bed chamber closed and her mam squeezed her hand. "I was so verra worried about ye, daughter."

Alisa took her other hand. "We just now heard that ye were awake." She shivered, "I canno' imagine what 'twas like for ye there in the dungeon."

Her mam's lips tightened. "I kenned all along that Lady Chisholm had something to do with it."

"And now Lady Alice is missing," Alisa said.

"What!"

CHAPTER TWENTY

DANIEL ENTERED THE great hall where the king was holding court with his entourage and some of the clan members. He looked up as Daniel approached him.

"It is time you made your appearance. Nobody will tell me anything except that ye have chosen Lady Beth Munro to marry but for some reason you didn't marry on Beltane as my order stated."

Daniel had to keep from smiling since the man sounded like a spoiled bairn. He bowed to the monarch. "My sincere apologizes, Yer Majesty."

The king drew himself up. "I wish to hear the story, Laird. I've heard all sorts of rumors, plus I was subjected to watching you carry Lady Beth in your arms up to her bedchamber and I must say she did not look well."

Daniel added food to his trencher from the platters on the table. He took a sip of ale and addressed the king. "I think Lady Chisholm was much more interested in me choosing Lady Alice for my wife than the lass was herself. I found Lady Chisholm very pushy and annoying. She continuously dragged Lady Alice around the keep, thrusting her in my path."

"I tried to have conversations with the lass, but she is verra shy and had no interests that she shared with me."

He stabbed a piece of meat with his eating knife and placed

the venison into his mouth. When he finished, he said, "Lady Beth and I have a great deal of common interests."

"If ye found Lady Chisholm so annoying, why didn't you just tell the woman ye had selected Lady Beth and set up the wedding as I had ordered?"

Daniel smiled and took a gulp of ale. "Ah, it seemed Lady Beth was reluctant to marry so I had to do some persuading."

The king sat back in his chair and raised his eyebrows. "Ye mean to tell me I ordered two lasses here so ye could select one and neither of them were willing to marry ye?"

Put that way, the situation did sound odd.

He grinned at the king. "Aye, I'm afraid so. I am no' the wonderful catch ye thought I was."

The king shook his head. "All ye had to do was order one of them to marry ye by Beltane and be done with it."

Daniel smiled to himself, thinking of how receptive Beth would have been to receive an order to marry him. "I believe one of the ladies likened the situation to me, picking one of them as I might a horse, yer majesty."

The king frowned at this, his eyebrows lowering, then raising as finally, he nodded. "Ah. Well. I see." He paused. "I choose not to be offended by that remark." Then he finished the rest of his ale and waved to one of the maids to re-fill it. "I am bringing Lady Chisholm with me to the palace and have her tried for treason."

Daniel swallowed his ale, knowing the punishment for treason. As annoying as he found the woman and what she'd done to the lass he loved, he wasn't happy to know she might be hanged.

"I will be sending Lady Alice back to her home with Lord Chisholm."

"Is Lord Chisholm no' going with his wife to the palace, then?"

The king grinned. "He said it was important for him to be with his clan because of issues they'd been having. I think he might find his wife as annoying as ye did."

Daniel finished his ale and thought about whether he should

tell the king that Lady Alice would not be returning with her da because she was missing.

BETH HAD LISTENED to her mam and Daniel argue for as long as she cared to listen. She was tired, her belly full for the first time in days, and they were busy arguing about the wedding.

Daniel was all for dragging Father Matthew up to her bedchamber right then, having the man marry them and then—as Daniel had said—"Be done with it."

That statement had raised her mam's hackles. "Laird or no laird, I willna allow my daughter to be married in her bed with her nightgown on. Lady Grant and I can have a wedding ready for tomorrow."

"I doona wish to leave Beth alone. She is upset after her ordeal and needs some comfort."

"If there is any comforting going on, my wife will be the one to do it." Lord Munro had entered the room, along with Lord Grant.

Daniel ran his fingers through his hair. Of course, as Beth's parents they had the right to protect her reputation. But the look on the lass's face with her da ordering Daniel out of the room twisted his insides.

"I understand, my lord. I will leave ye all now and return to my bedchamber for a good night's sleep before our wedding tomorrow."

Beth looked at him, panic in her eyes, but he winked at her and left the room.

Later, Daniel sat in his bedchamber, sipping on a glass of whisky, thinking about Beth and their life together which would start the next day. He smiled, imagining their disagreements and the great time they would have, making up.

He also pictured many lasses with her beautiful blond hair

and lads with his fiery red hair. Yes, life with Beth would be the best thing that could happen to him.

After enough time had passed and he'd heard Lord and Lady Munro and Lord and Lady Grant return to their bedchambers, Daniel downed his whisky, walked to his solar and pressed his hand against one of the walls. An area large enough for a man to pass through opened, and he slid through.

He walked along the quiet, dusty area and, after counting in his head, placed the candle he carried on the ground and pushed on the stone wall in front of him.

The panel opened and he blew out the candle and walked into Beth's bedchamber.

She sat up, pulling the bedding up to her eyes, wide and frightened. Then she smiled.

Her mam was in a chair next to her bed, asleep and looking very uncomfortable. Beth raised her finger to her lips, and he slipped back into the passageway.

"Mam, I think ye should go back to yer bedchamber. I'm fine now."

The woman opened her eyes, yawned, and looked relieved. "Are ye sure, Beth?"

She nodded. "Aye. Ye needn't stay here anymore."

Her mam stood. "If ye really think so."

Beth stretched. "Aye. I'm about to fall asleep."

"Then I will say good night and see ye in the morning, for yer wedding." She leaned over and kissed her daughter on the forehead.

Once he heard the door close, Daniel entered the room and stopped to stare at his bride.

She sat in the bed, so small in the large space. She was thinner, and dark circles appeared under her eyes from her ordeal. But to him she looked beautiful.

He crossed the room and threw the lock on the door, then made his way to her bed, unbuttoning his *léine* as he moved toward her. "I said I would ne'er leave ye."

He removed all his clothes, then climbed into the bed next to her, swiftly removing her nightgown. He studied her face. She appeared more relaxed, but very tired, so he put his plans aside and gathered her into his arms.

"Sleep, my love. I will be here all night."

CHAPTER TWENTY-ONE

A SOFT KNOCK on her bedchamber door awakened Beth. She looked frantically around the room, but Daniel was gone. "Enter," she said.

"Why was yer door locked?" Her mam asked once Beth had opened the door. "I thought ye said ye dinna need anyone to stay with ye."

"Um, I was a bit nervous so I decided a locked door would be best."

Her mam shook out a dress she carried with her. "Ye should have come and got me."

Eager to change the subject with her face flushing, she left the bed and was thankfully surprised to find herself in her nightgown. *God's bones*, she'd been tired. She never felt Daniel putting her nightgown back on.

"What is that?" she asked her mam as her sister entered the room.

"'Tis yer wedding gown. The ceremony has been set for ten o'clock. Yer cook has been busy making special food for ye and the Laird."

Even though she was absolutely certain she wanted this, Beth stomach tightened at the idea of marriage since she'd been against it for so long.

Then she pictured Daniel as he went against her mam to

insist on staying with her when Emma began her treatment and had to remove all her clothes.

Yes. This was definitely the right decision. She loved the man and he loved her. They would have a good life together.

Once she was washed, dressed, fussed with, and approved by her mam, the three of them left the bedchamber just a few minutes before ten o'clock.

As she made her way across the great hall to the kirk to be married, her da stepped up and took her arm. He smiled at her in such a way that tears welled up in her eyes. Within seconds the king moved to her other side and they three of them walked up to Father Matthew.

Although she was sure she was one of only a very few women who had the king walk her to the priest, all her concentration was on Chief of the Mackenzie Clan, Laird Daniel Mackenzie. Dressed in his formal attire, he made her feel a little dizzy. This amazing man, who loved her, rescued her and defied the king for her was soon to be her husband.

He reached out and took her hand and she immediately relaxed. They both turned to Father Matthew who glowed with happiness himself and began the ceremony.

DANIEL ENJOYED THE celebration of his wedding in the great hall, and didn't even mind that a great deal of the attention usually focused on the bride and groom was instead focused on His Majesty, King George II. He was sure almost every clan member was seeing the king for the first time and truly, not everyone had a king as a guest at their wedding, so he and Beth could be proud.

And the rest of the guests could all admire the king; Daniel spent his time admiring his beautiful wife and hoping she would soon tire of the celebration and let him bring her to his bedchamber where he planned another sort of celebration.

They'd had a wonderful feast that had him wondering how his cook Jemima was able to put together such a meal in what little notice she'd been given.

There had been hours of dancing, singing, and toasting the newly married couple.

He turned from watching Beth on the dance floor as Gregory slapped him on his back. "I figured yer new wife would no' want to have the traditional bedding ceremony so I passed the word among the verra drunk men that they are no' to start one."

"Aye, drunk or no', there is no way I want my men seeing my naked wife."

Lord Grant returned Beth to their table after a rousing dance. Daniel looked at her. "I want more than anything to bring ye upstairs and settle for the night, but I honestly do believe y'er looking a tad tired."

Beth smiled and touched his arm. "'Tis true, I am feeling worn out." She leaned in closer and said, "And 'tis anxious I am to see how ye plan to settle me for the night."

The smile she gave him had all his blood pooling in one place. Out of respect, Daniel turned to the king sitting next to him. "Yer Majesty, after my wife's ordeal, she is feeling tired, so we will retire now. I will speak with ye first thing in the morning."

The king smirked and said, "I don't expect to see you too early."

"Most likely no'," Daniel replied with a grin.

The king laid his hand on Daniel's arm. "I have sent Lady Chisholm and her maid to Kensington Palace where they will remain until Lady Chisholm's trial. I am no' yet sure what punishment would fit what the maid did."

He took a sip of ale and continued. "I will leave the lad, Joshua, in your hands to do what ye think is appropriate for his punishment."

Daniel nodded and then helped Beth up. He ignored the few calls from the men who were sober enough to start the bedding ceremony. He just laughed and shook his head and hustled his wife upstairs.

They entered his bed chamber. It was set exactly as he had requested. Flowers had been scattered on the bed, a bottle of wine stood on a table with pieces of the cake that Jemima had made for the wedding that they would have missed.

Beth turned to him, tears in her eyes. "This is beautiful."

He took her face in his hands and looked into her eyes. "Aye, but no' as beautiful as ye." He bent his head and kissed her, thanking God that he had this wonderful woman for his wife, and that she had survived the horror Lady Chisholm had put her through.

⫸⫷

SHE LEANED INTO his touch, heart thudding as he brushed his thumbs across her cheeks.

"I thought I would feel different as a wife," she whispered.

Daniel arched a brow. "And do you?"

Beth nodded. "I feel… safe."

His breath left him in a quiet rush, and then his mouth was on hers—warm, deep, full of love and hunger he'd held.

Her hands slipped beneath his shirt, sliding over the hard planes of his chest. He made a low sound and pulled her closer, lifting her into his arms and carrying her to the bed as though she weighed nothing.

Their bodies remembered the rhythm from their one time together, the heat, the way they fit—but tonight was different. He undressed her slowly, reverently, his lips following the path of each loosened fastener, each bared inch of skin.

"You're beautiful," he murmured against her collarbone. "And you're mine."

She tangled her fingers in his hair, pulling his mouth back to hers. "Only yours."

Their joining was a slow claiming, a deep, aching union that spoke more than words ever could. He moved within her with care, with reverence, his forehead resting against hers as their breaths mingled.

"I love you," she whispered as her body arched into his.

Daniel stilled, his breath shuddering against her skin. "Say it again."

"I love you."

He kissed her hard, and then again, his movements growing more urgent now, as if those words had unlocked something inside him he could no longer contain. She clung to him as pleasure rose between them, fierce and consuming.

When they finally came undone, it was together—bound in love and vows and a future neither of them would face alone.

EPILOGUE

Three months later

DANIEL HELD BACK Beth's hair as she brought the contents of her stomach up into the chamber pot. She hadn't had the time to make it to the garderobe, which happened most mornings.

She found it hard to believe that with her reluctance about a bunch of bairns, they had managed to start one of their own after only a couple of weeks of marriage.

He handed her a piece of linen and a glass of water. She smiled her thanks and wiped her mouth, then swished the water around and spit it into the chamber pot.

Daniel helped her up. "I'm sorry ye have to go through this, sweetheart."

She gave him a soft smile and they headed to the great hall to break their fast, although all she'd been able to get down in the mornings was a cup of tea.

Emma walked by their table. She stopped in front of them. "How is the new mam this morning?"

Beth shrugged. "My stomach is no' doing so well."

Emma smiled. "Aye, as I told ye, this will pass. Just give it a couple of more weeks. And make sure ye get enough rest."

The young woman hurried away from them.

"I wonder why such a young and pretty lass is no' married," Beth said as she watched Emma leave.

"She is too busy taking care of everyone else to think about herself," Daniel said.

Joshua appeared at the door to the keep and walked up to the laird. "My laird, I have a message here for Gregory, do ye ken where he is?"

"Nay, but I ken he will join us to break his fast. Ye can leave it here at the table."

When the lad nodded and walked away, Daniel looked at Beth. "'Twas verra nice of ye to not have me ban the lad from the clan, which I thought was an easy punishment for his part in yer kidnapping."

"I ken ye weren't happy about my decision, but I would have died in that dark cold place if Joshua dinna bring me food and make me eat it when I grew weak." She smiled at him. "I've wondered how long Lady Chisholm would have left me there were it no' for Joshua." She shivered.

Gregory joined them at the table. Daniel nodded to the piece of parchment on the table. "There is a message there for ye."

He took a seat and opened the message and read the words. His eyes grew wide and he shook his head, reading the document over again. "I canno' believe it."

"What is it?" Daniel asked.

Gregory ran his fingers through his hair. "I ken ye heard me speak of Robert Sinclair? We trained together at Dornoch Castle years ago."

Daniel nodded. "Aye. I remember ye speaking of him and I also remember him stopping by one time for a visit."

Gregory shook his head again as if clearing his brain. "He was killed in a minor skirmish on one of the Sinclair borders."

Beth's hand flew to her mouth. "Oh, my. How terrible."

"Aye," Gregory said. He turned to Daniel, "I will need to go to Castle Girnigoe."

Daniel frowned. "'Twill be much too late for the funeral. 'Tis a four or five day trip up there."

Gregory sighed and stared into space for a minute. "I ken

that, but there is another problem."

"Aye?"

"We made a vow to each other that if one of us died, the other would marry his widow, if he was no' already married."

He stared at the paper again. "I need to go fetch my wife."

THE END

Thank you for reading *A Highlander's Bride*. I hope you enjoyed Beth and Daniel's story as much as I have. Please join me in Gregory and Megan's story, *A Highlander's Vow*, coming in 2026. If you'd like to know more about it, or any of my other books or upcoming releases, please go here: calliehutton.com/newsletter to join my newsletter.

If you enjoyed *A Highlander's Bride*, please remember to leave a review. Reviews keep me writing!

Thank you,
Callie

About the Author

USA Today bestselling author, Callie Hutton, has penned more than sixty-eight historical romance books and Victorian Cozy Mysteries with humor and "historic elements and sensory details." (The Romance Reviews). Ms. Hutton's cozy mystery book, The Sign of Death was a finalist in the Simon and Schuster Mary Higgins Clark award in 2022. With close to a million novels sold and translated into several languages, she continues to entrance readers with her heartfelt stories.

www.calliehutton.com
facebook.com/calliehuttonsbooks
instagram.com/p/DEfvx2vOJ4S

9 781969 349553